How bad could it be?

"Why don't you hang out on Eyeball Alley with us tomorrow?" Lacey said.

I stared at her. Eyeball Alley is a hall in the back of the junior high with benches along the sides. The popular people sit on the benches and watch everyone else go by. I couldn't believe that Lacey was actually inviting me to join her there—to be one of the people who sat on the sides.

"I'd—I'd like that a lot," I said finally.

Lacey smiled and popped the fry into her mouth. "It's really fun," she said. "This morning some girl showed up wearing white pants and a white jacket. Can you believe that? So Justin said, 'Hey, it's the Good Humor man! Ding! Ding!' and everyone else yelled, 'Ding! Ding!' and the girl ran into the bathroom to hide. It was *so* funny."

I laughed, even though the story didn't sound that funny to me. It sounded . . . well, it sounded kind of mean. But maybe you had to be there to get the humor. Besides, all the most popular kids sat on Eyeball Alley. And I wanted to be popular.

"I'll be there," I promised.

One 2 Many

Written by
Jamie Suzanne

Created by
FRANCINE PASCAL

BANTAM BOOKS
NEW YORK • TORONTO • LONDON • SYDNEY • AUCKLAND

To Alice Elizabeth Wenk

RL 4, 008-012

ONE 2 MANY

A Bantam Book / March 1999

*Sweet Valley Junior High is a trademark of
17th Street Productions, a division of Daniel Weiss Associates, Inc.*

Conceived by Francine Pascal.

*Produced by 17th Street Productions,
a division of Daniel Weiss Associates, Inc.
33 West 17th Street, New York, NY 10011.*

ISBN: 0-553-48604-7

Published simultaneously in the United States and Canada

*Bantam Books are published by Bantam Books, a division of Random
House, Inc. Its trademark, consisting of the words "Bantam Books" and
the portrayal of a rooster, is Registered in the U.S. Patent and Trademark
Office and in other countries. Marca Registrada. Bantam Books, 1540
Broadway, New York, New York 10036.*

PRINTED IN THE UNITED STATES OF AMERICA

OPM   0 9 8 7 6 5 4 3 2 1

Jessica

"Jessica! Breakfast!" my mom called up the stairs on Monday morning.

Ugh. Maybe I can pretend to be sick, I thought.

I rolled over in bed and stared at the ceiling. It's not like I'm usually psyched to go to school, but today I was positively dreading it.

My twin sister, Elizabeth, and I had just transferred into a new school, Sweet Valley Junior High. So far, I hated it. The people there were totally unfriendly—especially the It crowd. Not that I expected everyone to just rush up to me, wanting to be my friend, but . . . well, why hadn't they? I mean, people at my old school, Sweet Valley Middle, had been dying to be seen with me. I wasn't used to having to make an effort to get people to like me. I wasn't used to not having any friends either.

What I needed was a crowd to hang with— quick. So last week I'd spent all of my time trying to hang with the most popular girl in the eighth grade, Lacey Frells. And she'd treated me like the plague.

But wait—it gets worse.

Last Saturday, I ran into Lacey at the movies. She was with her boyfriend. And when my brother, Steven, came to pick me up, she assumed he was *my* boyfriend—*and I let her!* Ick— I'm feeling queasy just remembering the whole scene. I don't know why I did it. I guess I wanted Lacey to think I had an older boyfriend so she would figure I was cool and welcome me into the popular crowd.

Now the more I thought about going to school and facing Lacey, the worse I felt. I was actually breaking out in a cold sweat when my mom called up the stairs again.

"Jessica! You'd better get moving!"

I threw back the covers, sighing. I showered, got dressed, and went downstairs.

I was running late, and my mom had left me a plate of eggs that were already growing cold. I sat down and picked up my fork.

Steven sat across the breakfast table, reading the comics and laughing. Every time he laughed, he spit a tiny bit of scrambled egg on the table. He looked so completely *mindless* that I could barely concentrate on his brown eyes or thick brown hair or any of the things that would make

Lacey think he was a cool boyfriend. I shuddered at the thought. Oh, how had I ever gotten myself into this situation? Lacey was going to find out the truth—and I was going to be dead meat.

"Jess, are you okay?" my mother asked, coming out of the kitchen.

I gave her a weak smile. "I'm fine, Mom."

"Are you sure?" She looked concerned. "You look a little pale."

The temptation to say, "Well, actually, I do feel kind of fluish," and crawl back in bed was almost irresistible. But it was only the second week of school—I couldn't pretend to be sick for the rest of the year. So I said, "I'm fine, really," and carried my plate, untouched, over to the sink.

I totally zoned as Elizabeth and I walked to the bus stop. She didn't seem to notice anything was wrong—she just kept chattering. Obviously she doesn't hate SVJH as much as I do. Elizabeth had settled down right away. She has this pair of dumb friends, "El Salvador" and Anna, and together they've all joined the school newspaper—bor-ing! That's pretty much all Elizabeth ever talks about now.

I studied my twin as we slid into our seat on the bus. *Elizabeth fits into the SVJH scene so*

3

well, I thought, *maybe I should ask her advice.* I felt kind of strange about asking, though. Elizabeth had never been more popular than me before. I took a deep breath.

"Lizzie?"

"Hmmm?" Elizabeth scribbled something in one of her notebooks.

"Have you ever—" I paused. "Have you ever told someone a lie or, well, not a lie, but a half-truth—not even a half-truth, but a misunderstanding that, um, got out of control?"

Elizabeth looked at me with a tiny line between her eyebrows. "What is this? A homework question?"

"No!" I said, exasperated. "This is my life we're talking about."

"Oh." Elizabeth looked thoughtful. "Well, just go to your friend and explain the misunderstanding."

That was such typical Elizabeth advice. I rolled my eyes. "It's not that easy," I told her. *And this isn't about a friend,* I thought.

"Well, what else can you do?" Elizabeth asked.

Switch schools, I thought. *Enlist in the army. Join the foreign legion. Run away with the circus.*

"Nothing." I sighed as the bus pulled up in front of the school. "I guess you're right."

As we walked up the sidewalk, I examined the sprawling, two-story, brown-brick building with small windows. The inside was kind of grimy, and the walls were painted a really obnoxious shade of yellow. I wished I were anywhere but here.

SVJH is pretty big—bigger than Sweet Valley Middle—so I figured it wouldn't be hard to avoid Lacey during the passing periods. This was a comforting thought. Maybe she would forget all about my "boyfriend" before I ever saw her again.

I said good-bye to Elizabeth and headed to my locker. I had planned to pick up all my books so that I could just slink from class to class during the day. But halfway down the hall I saw something that made my stomach practically fall out of my body: Lacey leaning against my locker, sneering at my locker partner, Ronald Rheece. He's the school's biggest nerd. Or smallest nerd, if you want to get technical.

I was just about to turn and run away when Lacey suddenly looked over at me . . . and *smiled.*

Gulp. I willed a smile to my lips, squared my shoulders, and walked up to Lacey. "Hi."

"Hi, Jessica," Lacey said. Her sun-streaked brown hair fell to her shoulders in waves. She

5

wore jeans and a pale blue T-shirt that brought out the icy color of her eyes.

"Hi, Jessica," Ronald squeaked. He looked kind of breathless. I'm sure he never thought Lacey Frells would be hanging out at his locker. Well, I never thought so either.

"I'm so sorry," he said to Lacey, "but I have to go now, or I'll miss my bus." He took a few steps backward, as though he could hardly bring himself to tear his eyes away from this vision. Then he turned and ran for his bus. It was a real Hallmark Hall of Fame moment.

Lacey looked after him with a frown.

"He takes a special bus over to the high school," I explained. "For some brainy math class."

"Oh," Lacey said, without much interest. Who could blame her?

I figured I'd better tell her all about Steven before I lost my nerve. *She's going to find out sooner or later,* I reminded myself. I opened my mouth to explain everything, and the bell rang.

"Come on," Lacey said. "Grab your books, or we'll be late for class. I can't wait till lunch!" she went on excitedly. "Then we can really talk."

I almost dropped the books I had just pulled off the shelf. Lunch? I'd been dying to sit at Lacey's table from the minute I got here. Eating

6

lunch with Lacey could be enough to change my whole life. I could be as popular here as I was at the middle school, maybe more!

I must have been staring at Lacey with my mouth open because she said, "Kristin's out sick, so you and I can sit together and talk about our boyfriends."

Boyfriends! I felt ill. I didn't want to dig myself any deeper into this lie.

Now is the time to tell her, I thought.

"I didn't see your boyfriend too well, but he looked pretty cute to me." Lacey smiled.

If I tell her, then she won't eat lunch with me, and I can kiss being popular good-bye. I didn't know what to do, so I just shrugged. I knew that Lacey could make things easier for me at SVJH. I also knew that she could make them harder.

Lacey swung my locker shut. "Let's go."

I swallowed. "Okay," I said weakly. *I can't tell Lacey the truth now,* I reasoned. *The halls are too noisy and crowded. I'll tell her at lunch, when it's just the two of us.* Yes, at lunch, definitely.

Without a doubt.

Or at the very, very latest by the end of the week.

Elizabeth

"En garde!" Salvador del Valle shouted.

He and my locker partner, Brian Rainey, were in the middle of a sword fight, using rulers that Ms. Upton passed out in algebra on Friday. They battled dramatically up and down in front of about half a dozen lockers. Unfortunately nobody who used those lockers could get to their books.

"*Touché,*" Brian yelled.

They both laughed but didn't stop clashing rulers and jumping around.

A small crowd formed. I glanced around at the faces and noticed Anna Wang standing alone near the edge of the group. I caught her eye and smiled. She cocked an eyebrow, stared deliberately at Salvador, looked back at me, and shrugged.

Anna and Salvador had been best friends forever. I felt really lucky to have met them my first day at SVJH. The three of us clicked right away.

Thinking about this made me wonder about *my* best friend, my twin. I knew Jessica wasn't crazy about SVJH so far . . . and she had acted sort of strange on the bus this morning. *I wish she could make friends too,* I thought.

Salvador gave a loud shout as he dodged one of Brian's sword thrusts, snapping me back to reality. With a jolt I realized it was getting late— and I still didn't have my books.

"Uh, guys?" I said, trying to make myself heard over Salvador and Brian's laughter. "Guys, a lot of people, including me, need to get to their lockers."

Salvador backed Brian up against one of the lockers and held his ruler to Brian's throat. "Surrendah!" he said in a phony English accent.

"Nevah!" Brian replied, knocking the ruler away. They started lunging and parrying all over again.

I rolled my eyes and looked back at Anna. She grinned at me. "Nice try. If you want to get their attention, I suggest you get out your ruler," she advised.

Fortunately the bell rang at that moment, and Brian and Salvador reluctantly ended their duel.

I crossed quickly to my locker, which was slightly ajar, and took out my books. I guess Brian already had his because he walked down the hall with just a quick wave and a "See you later, Elizabeth."

Anna and Salvador stayed behind to wait for me. "Boy," Salvador said as he slipped the ruler into his pocket, "these rulers are the best thing to happen at school since the cafeteria stopped serving meat loaf."

"Hey!" Anna protested. "I liked the meat loaf."

"Yeah, well, you like living dangerously," Salvador countered. He turned to me. "Did you know that last year two students collapsed after eating Chicken Supreme—which they also don't serve anymore—and the school tried to tell us that both kids had appendicitis? Nobody believed it, of course."

I laughed. "You're kidding, right?"

"No, he isn't. It was very suspicious," Anna added. "What are the odds of two attacks of appendicitis?"

"On the same day that they served Chicken Supreme?" Salvador demanded. "I'll tell you what the odds are! Zero! Less than zero! But the odds of food poisoning are—"

"Excuse me," said a low, throaty voice.

I looked up. Charlie Roberts was standing in front of us.

Charlie is the editor of the *Spectator*, the school newspaper, which Salvador, Anna, and I are all on. Charlie has really short, white blond hair and horn-rimmed glasses—she looks like an intellectual rock star. When I first met Charlie, I thought she was incredibly cool, but now that I'm getting to know her, I think she's very conceited. She's pretty intimidating either way, though.

"Hi, everyone," she said, smiling at the three of us. Her lipstick was so dark, it was practically black. "I've been looking for you, Elizabeth," Charlie went on. "I have a special assignment for you."

My heart rose. A special assignment? Maybe one of the other editors had had to drop out and she was going to choose me to be features editor or even photographer.

"What is it?" I asked eagerly.

"I want you to interview Mrs. Fransky," Charlie replied.

I had no idea who Mrs. Fransky was, but I didn't want to say so. Maybe she was a visiting dignitary of some sort.

"Okay," I said, trying to sound like I knew what I was talking about. "I'd love to."

"I'm afraid it's kind of a rush job." Charlie handed me a blue pass. "You can skip your second class and interview her then. She's in room two twenty-four."

I paused a moment, hoping Charlie would elaborate on the assignment. She didn't, though, and I would have felt like an idiot asking, so I said, "Sounds great," and swung my locker shut.

"I knew I could count on you," Charlie said. "You're so mature and reliable."

She gave us a cheery little wave and sauntered off down the hall.

I frowned after her. "Who is Mrs. Fransky?"

Salvador grinned. "All I can say is: Get ready for some close-range saliva spray."

"She's the home-ec teacher," Anna explained as we began walking down the hall. "She's about three hundred years old."

"And she's really boring," Salvador added. "You could interview her from now until Labor Day and not get enough interesting material to write a single paragraph."

I groaned. "Well, if she's just the home-ec teacher, I wonder why it's so urgent? Why did Charlie give me this pass and everything?"

"She's probably afraid Mrs. Fransky will get more boring with every passing minute," Salvador said.

Anna rolled her eyes. "Mrs. Fransky is retiring this year. Mr. Desmond probably told Charlie that the *Spec* had to run something on her in the first issue."

"Why choose me?" I asked. "I don't even know her."

"Because you're so mature," Salvador said.

"*And* reliable," Anna added.

I wrinkled my nose. "And this is my reward?" I flipped open my notebook as we walked. "Okay, you guys, I need help thinking up questions."

"Listen," Salvador said. "If you get her recipe for clam dip, you're going to be way ahead."

Jessica

"Do you want to see a picture of Gel?" Lacey asked, digging in her purse.

We were standing in the lunch line together, and even though I felt sick every time Lacey said the word *boyfriend,* I was pretty happy. Tons of kids walked by and said hello to Lacey. I smiled back at everyone. *Hello! Hello! Hello!* I thought. *Hello to my new life in the popular crowd!*

"Who's Gel?" I asked.

Lacey gave me an impatient look. "My boyfriend!"

"Oh," I said. "I thought you called him John at the movies."

"No, Gel."

Gel seemed like a pretty weird name, but I didn't want to say so. "Is that short for Angelo or something?" I asked carefully.

"No, everyone calls him Gel because he wears so much gel in his hair," Lacey said. She held out a photograph for me to examine: Lacey and Gel standing together on the beach. They were both very tan. Gel's hair did have a lot of gunk in it. In the picture he was leaning forward with his cheek next to hers, and part of his hair was touching her face. I wondered if she'd gotten hair gel all over her skin. It seemed kind of gross.

"What's your boyfriend's name?" Lacey asked.

"Steven Wake—," I said automatically. I realized what I was saying at the last second and coughed. "Steven Wakeman."

"Steven Wakeman?" Lacey repeated.

"Yes." I gave a nervous little laugh and wondered how I was going to pull this off. *Don't blow it, Jessica.* "Uh—we have almost the same last name," I went on. "That's how we met. At Happy Burger. They called our name and he picked up our order by mistake and I had to chase him out into the parking lot."

"Is he a sophomore?" Lacey wanted to know.

"Yes," I said. At least that much was true.

"I'll ask Gel if he knows him," Lacey said.

Yikes! "He doesn't go to Sweet Valley High," I said quickly. "He, um, lives just out of town, in another school district."

"Oh," Lacey said. "Well, do you have a picture of him?"

I did have a picture of Steven. I didn't really want to show it to Lacey, but she was looking at

15

me so expectantly that I shrugged. "Sure." I pulled out my wallet and showed her the snapshot I took of Steven last summer.

Lacey studied it. "Why is he crossing his eyes like that?"

"He always does that in pictures," I said.

"He does?"

Actually, yes, he does. It drives my mom crazy. We have a whole album of Steven looking like an imbecile.

"He thinks it's funny," I said. Then I had a great idea. "He's actually very immature," I added.

Lacey looked like she didn't doubt it.

"We might break up," I confided. "Soon."

Why hadn't I thought of this before? I could tell Lacey that we'd broken up at the end of the week. By then Lacey would like me and it wouldn't matter if I had a boyfriend or not. And I wouldn't ever have to tell her the truth.

Lacey and I reached the head of the lunch line. I had packed a sandwich, but since Lacey was having the hot lunch, I had decided to have that too. I asked for the spaghetti. Lacey got a hamburger.

She led me to an empty table. I had been hoping that we would sit at a table full of the most popular kids, but I was just as happy that

Lacey wanted to be alone with me. I knew the It crowd would still take notice.

"Listen, Jessica," Lacey said as soon as we sat down. She pushed her hamburger away, untouched. "I wanted to ask you, where do you tell your parents you are when you go out with Steven?"

A family reunion, I thought. "Oh, well," I said slowly. "I, um, say that I'm at a friend's house. Or the library."

Lacey smiled. "Yeah, I usually say I'm at Kristin's, but she doesn't like me to do that very much. You and I could say that we're at each other's houses. What do you think?"

My stomach was clenching like a fist now. That plan would get me busted in about two seconds. All I needed was Lacey calling my house to tell me to cover for her and my brother answering the phone. Still, I managed to smile at Lacey. "We could probably work something out," I lied.

Lacey toyed with a french fry. "What time do you get to school in the morning?"

"About seven-fifteen," I said. "Why?"

"Why don't you hang out on Eyeball Alley with us tomorrow?" Lacey said. "Kristin isn't allowed to talk on the phone when she's sick, so I don't know how bad she's really feeling. Her mom said she'd probably still be absent tomorrow, though. So there'll be plenty of room for you."

17

I stared at her. Eyeball Alley is a hall in the back of the junior high with benches along the sides. The popular people sit on the benches and watch everyone else go by. I had avoided it like the plague, not wanting to run the risk of someone making fun of one of my outfits. I couldn't believe that Lacey was actually inviting me to join her there—to be one of the people who sat on the sides.

"I'd—I'd like that a lot," I said finally.

Lacey smiled and popped the fry into her mouth. "It's really fun," she said. "This morning some girl showed up wearing white pants and a white jacket. Can you believe that? So Justin said, 'Hey, it's the Good Humor man! Ding! Ding!' and everyone else yelled, 'Ding! Ding!' and the girl ran into the bathroom to hide. It was *so* funny."

I laughed, even though the story didn't sound that funny to me. It sounded . . . well, it sounded kind of mean. But maybe you had to be there to get the humor. Besides, all the most popular kids sat on Eyeball Alley. And I wanted to be popular.

"I'll be there," I promised.

Salvador

"I have a problem," Elizabeth confided at lunch.

Lunch is the only period of the day that I understand. It's when you (*a*) eat and (*b*) sit around and chat with your friends. These are activities with obvious benefits. Unlike regular classes, in which you (*a*) drool on yourself in boredom and (*b*) can't get any sleep because the teacher keeps yakking at you. Plus lunch features the added benefit of getting to stare at Elizabeth, which is rapidly becoming my favorite hobby.

"What's the problem?" Anna asked, taking a big bite out of her apple.

Elizabeth finished chewing her BLT and swallowed. "Remember how Brian asked me whether we could stick all of our used chewing gum to the inside of our locker?" she asked.

"Oh yeah," I replied. "For some science experiment on growing mold, right?"

"Right. Well . . ." Elizabeth looked grave. *"It's working."*

"Ew!" Anna put down her apple and pushed it away. "Nasty!"

"Tell me about it." Elizabeth shook her head.

"What's nasty about it?" I asked. Both girls stared at me. "What?"

"Salvador," Anna said patiently, "there is something growing in Elizabeth's locker. That fact is disturbing."

Personally, the only thing I found disturbing about the situation was that Brian might get to spend time alone with Elizabeth working on a science experiment. *You and Elizabeth are just friends,* I reminded myself. *Just friends. Just friends. Just friends.*

"It's the miracle of life. I thought girls were into that stuff," I told them, knowing that comment would make one of them hit me. I was hoping it would be Elizabeth. "Ow!"

"That's for being a jerk," Anna said.

Elizabeth laughed, which made me happy because then I had an excuse to look at her. The sunlight was playing off her blond hair, and . . . well, I don't want to sound like a dork, but she looked like an angel. Believe me.

She glanced at me suddenly. "Is my hair doing something stupid?" she asked.

20

Her question caught me off guard. "No, why?"

"You're giving me this weird look." Elizabeth ran her hands through her hair, just in case, I guess. "Anna?" she asked. "Does my hair look weird? Be honest."

Anna looked carefully at Elizabeth. "You look great," she said finally.

I decided to change the subject before we could get into any sort of, "So then why was Salvador looking at me?" questions from Elizabeth. *Keep the staring under control,* I told myself. *Elizabeth is not interested in you as a boyfriend. Forget about it.* "What are you going to do about the gum fungus?" I asked.

Elizabeth sighed. "That's my problem. Brian is so nice. I feel bad telling him that his creation is grossing me out." She took another bite of her sandwich and chewed it thoughtfully.

"Just be honest with him," Anna advised. "You've got to get the gum out of there before it develops a mind of its own and turns on you."

"Yeah," I agreed. "Tell him to forget about the project. You can always work with someone else," I added.

"I know that's what I should do. I just feel awful about it." Elizabeth fiddled with her straw, then sipped her milk. *I will not stare at her lips. I will not stare at her lips. I will not—*

21

"Are you okay, Salvador?" Elizabeth's voice asked. I opened my eyes, and I was face-to-face with Elizabeth's mouth. She was leaning toward me, looking concerned.

"Fine," I squeaked.

"You've been acting really weird," Anna put in. "You didn't have the Chicken Supreme, did you?"

Elizabeth smiled at Anna. And that's when I saw it—Elizabeth had a piece of lettuce stuck in her teeth.

I was transfixed. *That lettuce is messing up the most beautiful smile ever,* I thought. It was just sitting there, in all its green glory, right on top of her front tooth.

I felt I had to do something about it, so I reached over . . . and *picked the lettuce out of her teeth!*

All three of us sat there, frozen solid.

Oh no, I thought.

I have never heard silence like that before in my life—I really believed I might die. *That's what I get for being so absorbed by Elizabeth's mouth,* I thought. I felt my face get hot and knew I was blushing like crazy.

Then Anna laughed. Quietly at first, then she started shaking until she was practically howling. Elizabeth stared at her, then she started laughing too. I still wasn't sure what to do.

"Uh—sorry about that," I said lamely.

Anna was wiping tears from her eyes, and Elizabeth was pounding the table. Finally Elizabeth pulled herself together enough to say, "So—so it wasn't my hair!" She collapsed into giggles again.

"Talk about gross!" Anna hooted.

"What do you mean?" I asked Elizabeth.

"All this time you've been staring at me and acting weird because I had a piece of"—Elizabeth laughed—"lettuce! In my teeth!" She took a couple of deep breaths, then grabbed my hand. About a million volts of electricity ran through my body. "Next time, Salvador, you can just tell me."

"Uh—," I said uncomfortably. "Okay."

She smiled her perfect smile. *Man, I have got to get myself under control or they're going to lock me up in the loony bin,* I thought.

Anna gave me a playful swat, and I turned to face her. "You idiot," she said affectionately. Then she grabbed my other hand. It felt warm and comfortable. No electric shock. "We're all friends. We can tell each other stuff like that."

I gave Anna a weak smile. She and Elizabeth both let go of my hands and leaned back in their chairs. I wondered why, if we were all friends, being near Elizabeth made me feel light-headed and being near Anna didn't make me feel any particular way at all.

Maybe it was because I didn't know Elizabeth that well, I reasoned. Maybe I just had to get used to being friends with her, like I was with Anna.

"Do you guys want to hang out Friday night?" I asked suddenly. "The three of us could do something fun, like go to a movie, or go bowling, or whatever."

Anna gave me a sideways glance. "You hate bowling," she said.

"I said, 'something *like* bowling,'" I countered. "As in similar to, but not exactly the same."

"It will be fun to hang out," Elizabeth put in. "Whatever we do. Maybe the two of you could come over for dinner one night this week too."

"Sounds great!" I said eagerly. *This is just so that we'll become better friends,* I told myself. *It has nothing to do with spending as much time as possible with Elizabeth.*

Nothing at all.

Jessica,

Ugh, this class is boring. I can't wait for school to be over so Gel and I can go to the mall. Do you want to come? Bring Steven.

Lacey

Lacey,

Steven and I can't make it today. He's sick. I was going to see if he wanted some chicken soup or something. Maybe some other time. How about next week?

Jessica

Jessica

"Steven, you can take my car today if you want," my dad said at breakfast the next day.

Steven beamed around a mouthful of fried eggs. "That'd be great, Dad." He looked at me. "Do either of you shrimps want a ride?"

"Not me," Elizabeth called from the kitchen, where she was packing lunches. "I have to be there early to set up another interview with Mrs. Fransky. I got *nothing* out of her yesterday. Jess, do you want an apple or an orange?"

"Um, apple," I called. "I don't want a ride either, Steven. I'm supposed to meet Lacey Frells on Eyeball Alley." Steven didn't know who Lacey was or how popular you had to be to sit on Eyeball Alley, and I was kind of hoping he'd ask.

Elizabeth came to the doorway. "*You're* going to sit on Eyeball Alley?"

"What's Eyeball Alley?" my mom asked, squeezing by Elizabeth and sitting down at the

26

table. Even my dad put aside the paper and looked interested.

"It's just a hall," I said nonchalantly.

"A hall where kids sit on the sidelines and insult everyone," Elizabeth said shortly.

My mother frowned. "That doesn't sound like a very nice club."

I rolled my eyes. "It's not a *club*, Mom. It's just a—thing. A place to sit."

"Well, it still doesn't sound very nice," my mom said.

"It isn't," Elizabeth told her.

I glared at my twin. "Elizabeth is making it sound worse than it is," I protested. "It's where all the *cool* people sit."

"*Oh,*" my dad said in a mock-impressed tone. "Well, if it's where the *cool* people sit, it must be okay."

Don't you hate it when parents get all sarcastic?

"I have to change." I pushed back my chair.

I was still in my robe, although I'd already taken a shower, so I hustled up to my room. Last night I had laid out my favorite pair of jeans and a sleeveless white blouse. That was what Lacey wore on the first day of school. I figured that meant it would be a safe choice for Eyeball Alley.

I turned from side to side in front of the mirror. The white blouse set off my tan, and my hair fell in long, clean lines to below my shoulders. I decided I had nothing to worry about.

"Jess!" Elizabeth called from the bottom of the stairs. "Hurry up or we'll miss the bus!"

"Coming!" I shouted.

I paused just long enough to rummage around in my makeup bag for an old tube of lip gloss. I didn't really use this one much because it dried out my lips. It was the kind Lacey carried, though, so I dabbed a little on. Then a sweep of mascara—done. I gave my reflection one last smile and ran down the stairs to where Elizabeth was waiting. Grabbing my backpack from the hall table, I followed her out the door.

We were halfway down the block when I realized that I had forgotten both my history book and my lunch. But I didn't really care because I was far too happy to think about history and because I was sure I would be eating lunch with Lacey and my new friends.

Thirty minutes later, though, I was nervous as I peered down Eyeball Alley. What if Lacey had forgotten about asking me to meet her here? What if someone made fun of me as I walked by? What if—

"Jessica!" Lacey called, waving to me from one of the benches at the far end. She looked cool and pretty in a denim miniskirt and red blouse. I hurried over to her gratefully.

Eyeball Alley is actually a fairly short corridor with benches along both sides. One wall is glass and faces the south parking lot. As people come in the door, most of them take the "safe" but long route past the home-ec room to get to their lockers. But if you're one of the poor slobs who has art or music or who just happens to have a locker in the west wing, then you have to walk down Eyeball Alley—there's no other way to get where you're going.

"Hi," Lacey said warmly. She moved her books so that I would have room to sit.

"Hey, Jessica Wakefield!" a voice called.

I turned.

"Who's that?" Lacey asked.

I smiled and waved. "It's Sheila Watson."

Sheila was a girl I'd known vaguely at Sweet Valley Middle. Now she was sitting almost directly across the hall from me. I hadn't even realized Sheila had been rezoned into Sweet Valley Junior High. She and I had been partners once for a history project. We'd had to work at each other's houses a few times and always had a good time hanging out. If I'd known she was here, I could have hung out with her last week.

Now, of course, I didn't need her. I was hanging out with Lacey.

"Jessica, this is Justin Campbell," Lacey said

as I turned back to face her. She gestured to the boy sitting next to her. "Justin, this is—"

"Jessica Wakefield," Justin said. He had blond hair and green eyes. "I heard. It's nice to meet you, Jessica Wakefield."

"Hi, Justin." I sank down on the bench beside Lacey.

Justin smiled at me. He had a really nice smile. "Did you just move here, Jessica Wakefield?"

His voice was teasing, but he didn't sound mean. He wasn't in any of my classes, so I didn't know if he was popular or not. I guessed that he probably was.

I shook my head. "My sister and I got rezoned from Sweet Valley Middle."

"Cool," Justin said, as though I was a positive addition to the junior high. I grinned.

"Listen," Lacey said to me. "Did you do the history homework?"

"Yes," I said. "But I left it at home. Do you have the book with you?"

She did, and we began doing the homework together while Justin lounged next to us, making occasional low-pitched remarks that sent us into giggles. "Look at how pale that girl's legs are," he whispered.

Lacey laughed. "They're blinding me."

I giggled too, which I decided wasn't really mean. The girl couldn't hear us or anything. Besides, I cared *way* more about what Justin and Lacey and all the other cool people on Eyeball Alley thought of me than about some random girl's opinion.

I peeked at the other people sitting on the benches. One or two of them looked at me curiously, I guess trying to figure out who Lacey's new friend was. I smiled at a pretty redheaded girl from my French class. She smiled back. Maybe I would sit next to her in class today. I spotted a cute boy from my swimming class and gave him a smile too. He winked. I wanted to jump up and down with happiness. I was going to be as popular as Lacey, I just knew it.

"What do you want to bet Mrs. Pomfrey collects the homework today?" Lacey said. "I'm never going to be able to answer all these end-of-the-chapter questions."

"I actually read the chapter," I said. "But it was so boring, I can't remember much."

"Well—as long as you remember at least a few of the answers—" Lacey broke off. "Oh, Jessica, your boyfriend's here!"

"Boyfriend?" I repeated, wondering for a second what she was talking about.

I followed Lacey's gaze out the window, where

31

I saw the most horrifying spectacle: Steven had pulled up to the curb outside.

My mouth went dry. *Oh no.* What was I going to do? I racked my brain quickly.

"Stay here," I said to Lacey. "I'll be right back." Fortunately we were sitting near a set of doors, and I hurried through them.

Steven was just opening the car door, but I waved to him and he closed it again. "You forgot your lunch," he said, holding it up.

"Thanks," I said quickly, taking the brown bag from him. I turned around to see if Lacey had followed me out, but she hadn't. I closed my eyes and let out a breath of relief. I still had to be careful, though. I was sure she was watching me from inside.

Then I had a brainstorm. Maybe I could turn this near disaster to my advantage. After all, Steven was here, and there didn't seem to be any danger of Lacey actually talking to him.

"Thanks a lot," I said again. I put my hand next to where Steven's elbow rested on top of the car door. From where Lacey was sitting, it would probably look like we were touching.

"No problem," Steven said. He put the car in gear. "See you later."

"Wait!" I said.

He looked surprised. "Wait for what?"

"I, um, want to tell you something," I lied.

"Well, tell me," Steven said.

I hesitated. "It's a secret."

"Okay."

I paused and then leaned forward so that my mouth was next to Steven's ear. What was I going to say? Then, remembering a story Elizabeth had told me before we went to bed last night, I whispered, "You have a piece of egg stuck in your teeth."

"Oh *no!*" Steven cried so loudly, he practically deafened me. "Do I really?" He tilted the rearview mirror and bared his teeth into it.

I straightened up. "See you later."

"I don't see any egg," Steven said.

"Bye." I stood back, and after another second of anxious looking, Steven pulled away from the curb. I waved.

Then I took a deep breath and turned back to face the school. I hoped the whisper had looked convincing. Let me tell you, I couldn't wait until Friday so I could tell Lacey all about my horrible ex-boyfriend and our heart-wrenching breakup. All of this pretending Steven was my cool older crush was enough to make me barf. I pushed open the glass doors.

Justin was looking at me admiringly from across the hall. "Who was that, Jessica Wakefield?"

I shrugged. "My boyfriend. He stopped by to bring me something."

Even Lacey looked impressed. I was sure that Gel never stopped by school in the mornings.

Then someone behind me let out a loud laugh.

I froze in the middle of Eyeball Alley. Even before I turned to face her, I knew who it was. Sheila Watson!

I turned around slowly.

Sheila was still laughing. "Jessica, what are you talking about?" she said. "That was your brother!"

I stood there, dumb, until she stopped laughing. She stared at me a minute. "Wasn't it?" she asked hesitantly. "Wasn't it your brother, Steven?"

I opened my mouth, but no sound came out.

"Is that true?" Lacey asked. I turned to face her again.

The hall suddenly seemed enormous and echoey. Everyone was staring at me. Two seventh-graders who had been walking by paused, clearly not wanting to get caught in the middle of anything. I swallowed, trying desperately to think of something to say that would save the situation. Nothing came to me.

"I'm sure it was your brother," Sheila said, clearly confused. She couldn't know that she was ruining my life, but I hated her all the same.

"He's, uh, he's . . ." I couldn't finish that sentence—or any other.

Lacey stared at me, her dark eyebrows raised. Then suddenly Justin snickered and whispered something in Lacey's ear. Lacey burst out laughing. "Nice going, Jessica *Lame*field," she said to me.

Everyone on the benches laughed. "Hey, Jessica *Lame*field!" someone called. "Does your sister date your brother too?"

I found my voice. "He's not my brother!" I cried, but I knew nobody would believe me. It was far too late for that.

"Jessica *Lame*field!"

"Lamefield? More like *Pathetic*field!"

"So that really was her brother?"

"Did you see her lean down and kiss him?"

Jessica Lame*field* . . . Lame*field* . . . Lame*field* . . .

Laughter filled my ears until I felt light-headed.

Lacey sneered, "I'd stay away from Eyeball Alley from now on, Lamefield! You would've been history once Kristin came back anyway."

The two little seventh-graders gave up. One ran toward the music room and one ran the other way, toward the doors.

And me? I ran into the bathroom and stayed there until the bell rang.

I wished that I could stay there forever.

Salvador

It was volleyball day in gym. Whoopee.

Elizabeth and Anna and I were on the same team, and we went way to the back where we could talk. Only Bethel McCoy can hit the ball that far anyway, so there was basically no danger of us having to actually participate as long as we cheered once in a while and looked alert.

"Salvador, you're the greatest," Elizabeth said.

"What did I do?" I asked, thrilled to have done it, whatever it was.

"You told me to get Mrs. Fransky's clam-dip recipe. I just reinterviewed her last hour and—"

"Look out!" Anna cried suddenly. "Bethel just hit the ball."

The volleyball whizzed straight toward Elizabeth, and she slammed it off her wrists. The movement caused her long hair to bounce and shimmer. All I could think was, *Beautiful, beautiful, beautiful . . .*

Snap out of it! I told myself, and cast a guilty

36

look at Anna just as the ball flew back to our side. Bethel must've gotten to it again. Anna held out her wrists, but the ball bounced off her forearm, smacking the head of someone from our own team, who said, "Ouch!" very loudly.

"Oops, *sorry!*" Anna called. She bit her lip and shrugged.

I felt even guiltier after seeing Anna look so klutzy, so I said quickly, "What were you saying about clam dip, Elizabeth?"

"Well, Mrs. Fransky told me how she invented the recipe," Elizabeth said, "and it was actually an interesting story."

Anna and I stared at Elizabeth in disbelief, and she made a face.

"Well, *fairly* interesting if you cut most of it out," she added. "Anyway, I'm not saying that it's Pulitzer Prize–winning stuff, but it's better than I expected."

Anna flipped her braid over her shoulder. "But she never gives that clam-dip recipe to anyone! It has this top-secret ingredient or something."

"Well, she gave it to me," Elizabeth said. "Since she was retiring and everything."

"*Is* there a secret ingredient?" Anna asked.

Elizabeth nodded. "Chocolate syrup."

Anna and I burst out laughing, and so did Brian, who was standing near us.

"What are you laughing about?" Miss Scarlett, the gym teacher, interrupted suddenly.

"Nothing," Anna muttered.

"Go, team!" I shouted, and Elizabeth clapped like crazy. Usually Miss Scarlett doesn't get mad if you show some enthusiasm.

"For your information," Miss Scarlett said slowly, "the game ended about thirty seconds ago."

"Oh," I said. "Did we win?"

"No," Miss Scarlett said. "Bethel's team won, as usual. I want to see you three in my office right now. You too, Brian."

She turned and walked toward the corner of the gym. We exchanged glances and followed.

"Do you think we'll get detention?" Elizabeth whispered. "I—oh, sorry," she said as she bumped into a guy named Matt Springmeier.

"Watch where you're going, Lamefield." He sneered and walked off.

Elizabeth stared after him. "What did he call me?"

Anna and I shook our heads, and Brian looked puzzled. We reached Miss Scarlett's office and paused in the doorway.

"Come on in," Miss Scarlett said, smiling unpleasantly. I wrinkled my nose at the Lysol-scented air.

We went in . . . barely. Anna actually kept a

foot outside the door, as though prepared to run. The girl's got brains.

"Now, since you four did not see fit to participate in the game today, I'm going to ask a small favor of you," Miss Scarlett said.

I looked at Elizabeth and Anna out of the corner of my eye. Was Miss Scarlett going to make us mow her lawn or something? Man, I hoped not. It seemed especially unfair to Brian, who had actually *been* playing and only laughed at the wrong moment.

Miss Scarlett reached into one of her desk drawers and pulled out an envelope. "I have been asked to find a team of volunteer dancers for the hospital dance-a-thon at the Sweet Valley Community Center this Friday." She turned the envelope over in her hands. "Do you know what's involved in a dance-a-thon?"

We shook our heads.

"For every hour you dance without stopping, five dollars will go to charity." She smiled again. "It will make up for the exercise you missed by not playing today."

"But Salvador, Elizabeth, and I have a *Spectator* meeting this Friday," Anna said in a tiny voice.

"You may go after the meeting." Miss Scarlett held out the envelope. "The dance-a-thon goes all night."

"My curfew is ten-thirty," I said.

"I'm sure the hospital will appreciate however many hours you dance," Miss Scarlett said. "So what do you say?"

Anna and Elizabeth didn't say anything. Neither did I, although my brain was racing.

Of course, it was Brian who reached for the envelope. He's too nice for his own good sometimes. "We'd be happy to go, Miss Scarlett," he said.

Oh, well. I guess we had a plan for Friday night.

A n n a

"So, how was school today?" my dad asked at dinner. We were eating kimchi, my favorite. My mom is an excellent cook, even though she rarely ever does it anymore, ever since Tim.

"Okay," I told him.

"Anything interesting happen?"

I swallowed a mouthful of rice. I debated telling him about the dance-a-thon punishment and decided against it. Who needed a lecture on taking gym more seriously? "Um, not really."

My dad nodded, and we were all quiet. I looked sideways at my mom, who was pushing her food around. Sometimes she goes days without eating.

Dinnertime is when I miss my brother, Tim, the most. He used to talk all through supper, entertaining us and making us laugh and telling stories about his day. I remember, when I was little, I used to listen to Tim talk about how

41

rowdy everyone got in the halls at SVJH. I couldn't wait to go to a school with passing periods, as opposed to the grade school, where you just sit in your classroom. But when I finally got to junior high, nothing interesting ever seemed to happen to me, the way it had to Tim.

The doorbell rang, jarring me out of the memory.

"I'll get it," I said. "I'm done eating anyway. Great dinner, Mom." She looked up at me and smiled. It was a sad smile, though.

I carried my plate to the sink and went to the front door. It was Salvador. I wasn't surprised. He always comes by without calling.

"What's shakin'?" he asked.

"Hey, Sal." I stepped out onto the porch and closed the front door behind me. Salvador and I headed over to the old porch swing as usual.

He sighed and pushed off with his feet. We rocked back and forth on the swing, his feet on the floor, controlling the movement, mine dangling, going with the flow. We didn't say anything. Best friends don't have to talk all the time.

I closed my eyes and felt the evening breeze on my face. I was remembering a night like this, long ago, when Tim had taken me to the park. He warned me not to swing too high, but I wouldn't listen to him. I felt as though I could touch the treetops as I swung higher and higher. Tim yelled at me to stop, but I didn't. Then—and I still have no idea why I did this—I let go of the swing and flung my arms out wide. Suddenly I was falling . . . down, down . . . and I landed on the ground with a sharp pain in my arm. Tim rushed over to me and picked me up. He whispered soothing things in my ear to stop my crying as he carried me all the way home. . . .

". . . don't you think?" Salvador asked. I opened my eyes and looked at him.

"Sorry," I said. "I think I was half asleep. What did you say?"

Salvador rolled his eyes. "Nice to know you care."

"It's not that," I protested, "it's just—"

"Easy, easy, Anna." He looked at me carefully. "I was just kidding. Since when are you so touchy?"

I blew out a breath. "I'm not, I just—I just want to know what you said, that's all."

"Well, now that I have your complete attention." Salvador gave an ahem. "I was just thinking about what it would take for us to get a special assignment on the *Spec,* like Elizabeth's. Maybe we could do something on the dance-a-thon. Maybe Elizabeth could convince Charlie that we're mature and reliable too. I wonder if Elizabeth would do that?"

Anna

I wondered why Salvador was saying Elizabeth's name every two seconds. Last week Salvador had ditched me to take Elizabeth to a concert, which had made me really mad. The thought that Salvador might be crushing on Elizabeth grossed me out. Anyway, he apologized for blowing me off and promised that nothing would change our friendship, which made me feel a little better.

And I know Elizabeth could never *like* like Salvador, but still. I can't help feeling a little jealous sometimes.

I cleared my throat. "I'm not sure that the dance-a-thon is newspaper material."

"But that's the challenge of it!" Salvador protested. "To take the most boring assignment ever and turn it into something interesting. Like Elizabeth's interview. Maybe she could turn that into a parody or something."

There he goes mentioning Elizabeth again! I thought, irritated. I didn't know why it was bothering me so much. I opened my mouth to say something like, "If you came over here just to talk about Elizabeth, I'll let you use the phone and you can give her a call," but Salvador cut me off.

"*You'd* be good at that, Anna," he said.

I frowned. "Good at what?"

He gave me a haven't-you-heard-a-word-I've-said look and explained, "At writing *parodies*. You're funny. You should submit one."

Salvador thinks I'm funny? I thought. *He'd* always been the funny one. I smiled at him. "Thanks," I said warmly.

"We could work on one together," Salvador said, turning to face me, "if you want."

I looked at his face in the dim light spilling out onto the porch from the living room. *Salvador is so handsome,* I thought, and the realization took me by surprise. We had been friends since kindergarten, but I don't think I'd ever really noticed the way he looked. And there was something about the way his face was tilted and about his expression . . . in those shadows, at that moment, Salvador reminded me of Tim. Suddenly I felt really sad.

Salvador seemed to notice and touched my hand. A wave of something—was it relief? Hope? I wasn't sure—washed over me.

I looked into his black eyes.

Salvador is your best friend, I thought. *He isn't going anywhere. If he had a crush on Elizabeth, he would tell you.*

"Okay," I told him. "That would be great."

One Time
by Anna Wang

One time
when my parents were away,
my brother and I
dressed the cat in a sweater
and put her in an old baby carriage.

All afternoon
we wheeled her around,
and whenever anyone
looked in the carriage,
my brother put his arm around me
and said, "Me and the missus
are awfully proud of our little one."

Things like this
should be mentioned at funerals,
but aren't.

Jessica

"Hi, Jessica Lamefield," some ugly boy said.

I was almost too tired and heartsick to glare at him. Almost. Lamefield! What a stupid nickname. If it hadn't been directed at me, I would have laughed in his face.

I walked into geography, which, as luck would have it, is one of those classes without a seating chart. I was going to have to try to find someone to sit next to, someone who wouldn't humiliate me.

Lacey—had I ever been happy that Lacey was in all my classes?—was sitting next to a friend of hers named Clarissa. As soon as they saw me, they looked at each other and burst into laughter. I felt my cheeks grow warm, although I should have been used to laughter like that by now—it had been happening all day.

I turned quickly and sat in the front row. I had planned to sit in the back, but now I didn't want to walk down the aisle. What if—what if someone tripped me? I squeezed my eyes shut. I wasn't used to having to think about stuff like that.

"Hi, Jessica."

The voice was friendly, and I opened my eyes. It was Ronald Rheece, looking at me with his big, brown puppy eyes. I'd forgotten he was even in my geography class. Usually I tried to put as much distance between us as possible so people wouldn't think we were friends.

Ronald sat down next to me, which actually made me happy. It was better than having nobody sit there.

Mr. Harriman gave us a pop quiz on world capitals (yikes), which took about half an hour. The whole time I could hear the rest of the class whispering, but I couldn't tell if it was about me or not.

Finally, when there were only ten minutes of class left, Mr. Harriman pulled down the map and asked if anyone wanted to come up and point out Patagonia.

Ronald's hand shot up immediately, of course, and Mr. Harriman called on him.

Ronald trotted to the front of the room and placed his finger on the map.

"Good," Mr. Harriman said.

Ronald sat down, reluctantly, it seemed to me. He probably wanted Mr. Harriman to ask him another question. I was so busy thinking about this that I didn't hear a word Mr. Harriman was saying until he asked, "Jessica?"

I jumped. "What?"

"Would you please come up and point out the Maritime Provinces on the map?" Mr. Harriman asked patiently.

I stared at him for a long, horrified moment and then slowly got to my feet and walked to the map. Behind me I heard a low giggle. I knew it came from Lacey.

"The, uh, what provinces?" I asked Mr. Harriman.

"Maritime."

I swallowed. I had no idea where the Maritime Provinces were. I looked at the map, and it suddenly seemed huge, much larger than ever before.

The swell of laughter from the classroom grew louder. "Lamefield," someone whispered, just loud enough to reach my ears. I glanced at Mr. Harriman, but he hadn't seemed to hear.

I guess only thirty seconds went by as I stood there, but it felt like ten hours.

"Here?" I said desperately, pointing at a place on the map near Asia.

The class laughed out loud.

"No," Mr. Harriman started, and turned toward

49

the class. "Will you be quiet?" he snapped. "What's so funny anyway?"

That only made everyone laugh harder.

Mr. Harriman banged the pointer against his desk. "Does anyone want to let Jessica and me in on the joke?" he asked.

The class fell silent, and I cringed. Having a teacher defend me was *worse* than being laughed at.

"Well?" Mr. Harriman asked.

I prayed that nobody would let him in on the joke. I took a quick peek at the classroom. It seemed full of jeering faces, except for Ronald. He was looking at me with pity and understanding— as though I was just like him.

Of course, I knew I wasn't.

After all, nobody had laughed at Ronald when he went to the map.

What Teachers Really Mean
by Salvador C. del Valle and Anna Wang

When teachers say . . .
> "Do you have something you'd like to share with the class?"

They really mean . . .
> "Please repeat whatever embarrassing thing you were saying."

When teachers say . . .
> "Are you paying attention?"

They really mean . . .
> "I lost my train of thought."

When teachers say . . .
> "Does anyone want extra credit?"

They really mean . . .
> "I have some yard work I need done."

When teachers say . . .
> "That's an interesting question."

They really mean . . .
> "I have no idea."

When teachers say . . .
> "What's so funny?"

They really mean . . .
> "Do I have food in my teeth?"

When teachers say . . .
> "Jason, will you watch the class for a few minutes?"

They really mean . . .
> "I have to go to the bathroom."

When teachers say . . .
> "Class will be dismissed ten minutes early today."

They really mean . . .
> "I need a cigarette."

When teachers say . . .
> "Today we're going to watch a video."

They really mean . . .
> "I need a nap."

When teachers say . . .
> "Please show your appreciation for our guest lecturer."

They really mean . . .
> "Clap or else."

Elizabeth

Anna and Salvador walked me to my bus after school. They do that pretty much every day now.

Salvador was studying the dance-a-thon tickets. "There's no way out of this," he announced. "I thought maybe we could get disqualified for being too young or too bad at dancing, but it says 'everyone welcome' about twenty different times."

"Well," I said cautiously, "we wanted to do something together on Friday anyway. And I think it sounds kind of fun."

"That's just because you've never been to a dance at the community center," Salvador countered. "I was forced to go to one a couple of years ago, and a high school *marching band* was the music. Do you know how hard it is to dance to 'Pomp and Circumstance'?"

Anna and I burst into laughter. I looked at Salvador, thinking, *He sure is cute*.

I stopped laughing. That wasn't what I meant to think at all. I had meant, *He sure is funny.* That's it. Funny.

"Hey, Anna," Salvador said. "We'd better let Elizabeth get on the bus. It's about to leave."

"Oh, okay," Anna said. She looked at me. "I think the dance-a-thon will be fun too," she said.

Salvador rolled his eyes. "You guys don't know what these things are like. Believe me, you'd have more fun getting down to the music at the dentist's office." But he was grinning. He had the cutest grin.

There I went again. I didn't mean cutest. I meant . . . nicest.

"Bye, Elizabeth," Anna said.

I nodded and climbed onto the bus, still thinking. Not cute. That wasn't the right word at all because Salvador wasn't cute. Well, I mean, maybe he was to some girls, but not to me. To me, he was just funny and friendly and nice and easy to talk to and interesting and . . . yes, he was all of those things, but not cute.

I was so busy thinking about this that it took me a long time to notice that my sister wasn't on the bus.

Jessica

I can't believe I'm hiding in the *bathroom*, I thought. *Again.*

I checked my watch. Two more minutes. Then I would dash to the bus, go home, and cry. After the second hand had swept around twice more, I eased open the door of my stall. Nobody was in the bathroom. I tiptoed to the exit and peered into the hall. Nobody was out there either, which was how I had planned it.

I left the girls' room and walked quickly down the hall to my locker. Ronald was already gone, but he had left the locker turned to the last digit of the combination, so it only took a second to open it.

I grabbed all of my books—who knew when I would feel like coming back to school? I piled my notebooks on top of the texts and was just reaching for my jacket when a voice hissed, "Jessica Lamefield!" right in my ear.

I was so startled, I dropped the whole pile of books.

I whirled around to see Justin Campbell. Another boy, Matt Springmeier, was with him. Their hands were behind their backs, and they were both grinning.

I leaned down for my books, glaring at them.

Justin laughed. How could I ever have thought Justin had a nice smile, or nice eyes, or a nice anything? He was the biggest jerk I'd ever met . . . and that was saying something.

"What are you guys doing here?" I asked. "Don't you ever go home?"

Justin flashed a mean smile. "We have an after-school project to work on," he said.

Matt laughed, and both guys brought their hands from behind their backs. They were holding cans of shaving cream.

I had a bad feeling about that, but I tried not to let it show. "What's the project?" I asked. "Are you going to shave each other's legs?"

Justin's smile faltered a moment, then recovered. "No, *Lamefield*," he said slowly, "we're going to redecorate your locker."

Oh no—they're going to squirt shaving cream into my locker! Most of my books were already out, but what about Ronald's stuff? It would be totally ruined. I really didn't want that to happen—not because Ronald was such a good friend of mine, but because he was the only person who had been nice to me all day.

Suddenly I was close to crying. I couldn't believe these guys were being so mean to me. I'd never been in a situation like this before. This was the kind of thing that happened to—to nerds and losers and people nobody liked. I thought about the sympathetic look Ronald had given me and lunged at Justin.

"Give me that!" I yelled, reaching for the shaving cream. Justin stumbled back a step, and Matt grabbed the opportunity to get to my locker. I tried to intercept him, grabbing at his can of shaving cream this time, but he jerked it away from me with a snarl. The sound surprised me, and I looked into his face in time to see his expression change from anger to confusion.

I turned and saw why. A tall guy had grabbed the can right out of Matt's hand. He had Justin's shaving cream too.

"Give those back," Justin demanded.

The tall boy gave him a look that shut Justin up fast. He turned to me and said politely, "Do these belong to you?"

I nodded and caught my breath as he handed me the shaving cream. "Thanks," I whispered. I tossed the cans in my locker and slammed it closed. *This has been the worst day of my entire life,* I thought. Then—I couldn't help it—I just started to cry. I was quiet about it, at least. The tears just slid down my face as I stood there, not knowing what to do . . . or think.

The tall boy looked at Justin and Matt again, which was enough to convince them to get lost. They took off down the hall—although I could tell they were trying to act like they weren't hurrying.

The tall guy collected my books and notebooks quickly and piled them in my arms as I kept my eyes on the ground, trying to pull myself together. I took a final deep breath and looked up at him. I didn't know what to say, so we stared at each other until he pulled a bandanna out of his back pocket and wiped the tears from my face.

"You still have time to catch your bus, I think," he said gently.

I couldn't believe this guy was being so nice. He didn't even know me! As I looked up at him again, a little flower of hope bloomed in my heart. Here was someone nice, someone *handsome,* someone who obviously wanted to know me. Who needed Lacey or the popular crowd when I had . . . him?

I managed a smile. "Thanks again."

He smiled. "No problem," he said, "Elizabeth."

I stared at him, openmouthed.

Elizabeth? *Elizabeth?* No wonder he had been so nice—he thought I was my sister! I should have known better than to think that anyone would stand up for Jessica Lamefield.

I felt tears welling up in my eyes again.

I turned and ran down the hall before he could see.

Elizabeth

I ran to the front of the bus and put my hand on the driver's arm just as he turned the ignition key.

"Wait!" I said.

The driver glared at me. "What's your problem, girlie?"

"My sister isn't here yet," I said. "Can't you wait a minute?"

"This bus leaves the school at two-thirty, no matter who's on it or who's not," he said, starting to pull out into traffic.

"There she is!" I said suddenly as Jessica flew out one of the school's front doors and began galloping across the lawn. "Can't you wait just a minute? Please?"

The driver looked irritated, but he waited. I stood next to him. I heard a lot of laughter as Jessica sped across the grass. I wondered why— hadn't any of these kids seen someone run for the bus before?

When Jessica got on the bus, she looked just awful. Her skin was red and blotchy, her hair stuck damply to the sides of her face, and her eyes were watery. She'd been crying, or close to it.

"I saved you a seat in back," I whispered. "Do you want me to carry some books?"

Jessica shook her head. I suddenly felt very self-conscious as we walked down the aisle.

A boy in one of the front seats whispered, "Lamefield!" in such a mean voice that I felt a flush creep up my neck. What was going on?

Jessica ignored him, and she continued down the aisle and slammed herself into the seat I'd saved for her, breathing heavily.

"Hey," I said gently, sitting down next to her. "What's wrong?"

Jessica waited until the bus was in motion. Then she put her head close to mine, held a notebook in front of our faces, and poured out the whole story. About Lacey and Steven, about Justin's nickname for her, and about how he and another guy had teased her at her locker.

As I listened, I began to feel as though a hot coal were burning just below my heart. I was furious.

I thought about Lacey Frells and the few times I'd seen her in the parking lot after school, talking to her greasy-haired boyfriend and

61

teasing the younger kids. Why did my sister always choose the most obnoxious people to be friends with? Why couldn't she pick people who were nice—and honest? Like Salvador and Anna, for example.

When we finally got to our stop, Jessica still looked so miserable that I said, "Let's go to I Scream." That's the ice-cream parlor near our bus stop.

"I don't have any money," Jessica mumbled.

"Well, I do," I said. "Come on, everything looks better over ice cream."

"Who are you, Mary Poppins?" Jessica asked. Then she seemed to reconsider. "Okay."

So we went to I Scream, where I had a mint–chocolate-chip cone and Jessica ordered a hot-fudge sundae. She didn't seem to have much appetite, though. Mainly she just stirred the sundae around and around until it looked like chocolate soup.

Finally Jessica put down her spoon. "I'm not going to school tomorrow," she announced. "I'm going to stay home sick."

"You'll have to go back sometime," I said. "You can't stay out sick for the rest of your life."

"Not even if I pretend to have mono?" Jessica asked.

"Come on," I coaxed. "How bad can it be?"

That was the wrong thing to say. Jessica's eyes filled up with tears. "You don't know!" she wailed. "You can't possibly imagine what it was like. It was horrible! The only reason that guy saved me was because he thought I was you."

"What guy?" I asked.

Jessica blew her nose on her napkin. "I thought I told you. This really muscley, cute guy who stopped Matt and Justin from spraying shaving cream into my locker. He thought I was you."

"Salvador?" I asked.

Jessica gave me a withering look. "I said *muscley* and *cute*. Besides, I know who Salvador is."

"Well, look," I said slowly, as an idea took shape in my mind. "Will you go to school tomorrow if I promise to stick by you the whole time? I'll walk you to all your classes—we can go everywhere as a twosome."

Jessica shook her head.

"Jessica, nobody would dare be mean to two of us," I said. "They won't even know which of us is you and which is me. Anna and Salvador can come along too. You'll have lots of protection."

Jessica appeared to think about it. "Maybe."

"Good," I said. "Let's go home."

At the doorway Jessica sucked in her breath and ducked behind me.

"What's up?" I asked her.

"Shhh!" she hissed. "It's Kristin Seltzer."

Oh no. Lacey's best friend. Was she going to say something mean to Jessica?

"She's coming over," Jessica moaned. She grabbed my hand and squeezed the life out of it.

"Hi, guys," Kristin said cheerfully, walking right up to us. Her curly, dark blond hair was like a cloud, and her wide blue eyes were friendly. She turned to the woman next to her and said, "Mom, this is Jessica and Elizabeth Wakefield. This is my mom."

I said hello politely, and Jessica sort of grunted. My heart ached for my twin, but Kristin didn't seem to be acting strange. Kristin looked a lot like her mom, except that her mom was very tall and thin—like a model. "I was out sick today," Kristin went on. "So don't tell anyone you saw me getting ice cream."

"What were your symptoms?" Jessica asked tentatively.

"Just a cold," Kristin asked. "Why? Are you coming down with something?"

"You never know," Jessica said darkly.

"Well, I hope not," Kristin said. "Because I think tomorrow is the day that Miss Scarlett gives her annual lecture on cold sores and you don't want to miss that."

"Oh, Kristin, for heaven's sake," Mrs. Seltzer said. "We're just about to eat."

"Well, it's true," Kristin said. "See you later."

"Bye," I said. Jessica nodded and relaxed her grip on my hand.

As soon as they went inside, I said, "See? Kristin was nice to you."

"She was out sick and doesn't know to hate me yet," Jessica pointed out bitterly. "Plus her mom was standing right there. Even a serial killer has to be nice to you if his mom is within earshot."

I couldn't really argue with that, so we walked the rest of the way home in silence.

Salvador

"Did Salvador tell you that we're going to a dance-a-thon on Friday?" Anna asked that night.

My grandmother—I call her the Doña—looked delighted. "A dance-a-thon? Is it for charity?"

I nodded miserably.

"Oh, that's wonderful, dear hearts," the Doña said. "Wait until I tell Mr. Fox." Mr. Fox is the Doña's dance teacher. "Oh, I know! Why don't I arrange a private dance lesson for you?"

"It's not that kind of dancing," I protested, but she was already gone. I could hear her in the kitchen on the telephone, and a minute later she appeared in the doorway, triumphant.

"Mr. Fox says we should come right over," the Doña announced. "He has a free hour."

I groaned. The only thing worse than dancing is dancing with my grandmother—especially if Anna was coming along as a witness. But the Doña's mind was made up. She flew up to her room to change and then hustled both Anna and me out to the car. She seemed very happy and was humming to herself as she started the engine. I noticed that she was wearing a dress and she even had on lipstick and some of that junk—what do you call it? Eye shadow?—on her eyelids. I had a funny feeling about the whole evening.

"Ah, Sofia," Mr. Fox said to the Doña when we arrived in the dance studio. "You look stunning, as always." He actually kissed her hand.

Anna moved closer and whispered in my ear, "He's not going to do that to me too, is he?"

I shook my head. "No, only the Doña gets that treatment."

"Thank goodness," Anna said. She stayed right by me, though, I guess in case Mr. Fox got any ideas.

The Doña put her arm around my shoulders. "You remember my nephew, Salvador," she said.

Mr. Fox held out his hand, but I started coughing so badly, I couldn't shake it. Nephew! I was the Doña's *grandson!*

The Doña thumped me on the back. "Are you all right?"

"Fine," I said, although my eyes were watering. "Fine, *Aunt* Sofia."

"And this is Salvador's friend, Anna," the Doña continued.

Anna shook hands with Mr. Fox too.

Then Mr. Fox said we should begin with a waltz since that was easiest. He said that he would teach me first.

Well, maybe the waltz is the easiest for some people, but not for me. Mr. Fox told me just to follow his lead. I guess he'd never led anyone like me before, though, because about two seconds later we crashed into the table holding the record player and the needle skidded across the record.

"Perhaps you and Anna should practice the box step," he suggested, straightening his ascot. He showed us how to follow these shoe prints that were painted on the floor.

"This looks pretty simple," Anna said hopefully.

"It had better be," I replied.

Mr. Fox whirled around the floor with my grandmother—or aunt, as the case may be—as Anna and I tried not to stomp on each other's feet.

I thought it would feel weird to dance with Anna, but it didn't. At least my hands didn't start sweating, which sometimes happens if I get nervous. Maybe it was because we were both staring at the floor, trying to follow the shoe prints, and it was more like dancing by myself. Besides,

Anna didn't really care if I stepped on her toes, and her hair smelled nice, like flowers.

"Hey," Anna said suddenly, "we just completed our first box step without either one of us getting out of step."

"How can you talk and count at the same time?" I asked. Immediately we messed up and had to start over.

"Sorry," Anna said. She gripped my hand a little tighter.

I smiled at her. I usually never thought about the fact that Anna was a girl, but I had to admit that sometimes it was convenient. Like now. I would have felt like a real dork dancing with one of my other friends. Brian, for example.

So Anna and I practiced the same four steps over and over in the middle of the room while the Doña and Mr. Fox swept around us, complimenting each other.

"You are light as a feather, Sofia."

"Oh, Alphonse, you're too kind."

When I heard the Doña say "Alphonse," I began laughing so hard that I completely lost track of my box step and practically killed Anna by causing her crash into one of the pillars.

"Are you okay?" I asked.

Anna blinked and rubbed her shoulder. "Yeah, I guess so. Are my pupils the same size?"

I peered into her eyes. "Yeah, why?"

"Because different-size pupils are the first sign of a concussion," she said.

"You do not have a concussion." I rolled my eyes. "Now, that guy you whacked with the volleyball today, he might have a concussion."

Anna laughed and took my hand. "Dance with me," she said. We began practicing again.

After we'd practiced—and the Doña and Mr. Fox had flirted—for about twenty minutes, Mr. Fox led me around the floor in a very simplified waltz.

"Ah, Sofia," he said to the Doña. "Your nephew shows great promise."

Why do adults lie like that when it's so obvious?

Then Mr. Fox led Anna around. Anna was actually a really good dancer, although Mr. Fox is about three feet taller than she is and the two of them looked pretty silly together.

When they had finished dancing, I shook hands with Mr. Fox and told him how much I had enjoyed the lesson (a lie) and that I would be back soon (another lie). Then I told him that he should dance with the Doña again because they were such a pleasure to watch (a third lie). The Doña and Mr. Fox pretended that they didn't want to dance with each for about three seconds, and then they started smiling. Mr. Fox put on a record and they spun around the room, the soft lights glinting off their silver hair. I don't think either one knew that we were there.

"Oh," Anna breathed. "This is so romantic."

I shook my head.

Girls.

Jessica

"I can't," I said to Elizabeth as the bus pulled up in front of the junior high the next morning. I gripped the edge of the seat in front of us. My stomach felt like it was turning inside out, and my mouth was dry. "I can't go in there."

"Yes, you can," Elizabeth said.

"No," I said, beginning to panic. "I'll just— just stay on the bus and go back to the garage with it."

"Jessica—," Elizabeth started.

"Hey," the bus driver said. "Are you girls getting off or not?"

"No!" I said quickly.

He glanced at us in the mirror. "Hey, you're the one who didn't want to get on yesterday and now you don't want to get off?"

"Don't worry," Elizabeth said to him. "We're going."

"See?" I whispered. "Even the bus driver is mean to me!"

"He's mean to everyone," Elizabeth said. She pried my fingers off the seat in front of us. "Come on, Jessica."

I grabbed Elizabeth's arm as we walked up to the school. "You promise you won't leave me?"

"Not even for one second," Elizabeth said calmly. "It'll be fine."

So we went inside and walked down the halls together, practically in lockstep, as though we were Siamese twins instead of identical ones.

First we went to Elizabeth's locker, where her totally cute locker partner, Brian Rainey, cocked an eyebrow at us and said, "Which one of you is the evil twin?" in a way that made even me laugh.

Then we went to my locker, where *my* partner, Ronald, told us that identical twins have the same fingerprints. Obviously it didn't make us laugh. It did make me want to strangle Ronald, though.

Then we headed toward my first class, and although I cringed every time someone passed us, nobody called me "Jessica Lamefield." I knew that nobody would've forgotten about it—a nickname like that could follow you around forever. But maybe not as many people knew about it as I had thought. Or maybe they were too afraid to do it when they couldn't be sure which one of us was which.

In fact, I think everyone was realizing for the first time that we were twins. A few people did a double take or said really stupid things like, "Are you identical twins?" and "Can you use each other instead of a mirror?" But tons of kids just laughed and said, "Hey, twins! Cool!" Also, a lot of kids said hi to Elizabeth. *Sticking by her side could be the best thing that ever happened to me,* I thought. *Elizabeth's way more popular than I ever realized.*

I began to relax just the tiniest bit.

Elizabeth waited with me right outside my first class. She promised to stay until the bell rang.

"How are you doing?" she asked me.

I shrugged. "Better than I expected. I mean—" But then I looked up and froze. Lacey was walking toward us with a nasty smile on her pretty pink lips.

"Hey, Lamefield," she said. She came right up to us. "Are you going to hide in the bathroom during lunch again today? Why don't you come into the cafeteria?"

I knew as well as the next person that the worst things always happened in the cafeteria, where the teachers weren't around. Chairs pulled out, milk spilled, food thrown, feet stuck in aisles—the cafeteria was the most dangerous place if you were unpopular. Besides, Elizabeth didn't have the same lunch I did. There would be no wonder twin power to protect me.

Elizabeth had opened her mouth to say something to Lacey but seemed to change her mind. She turned slightly and said, "Hi, Kristin!" in a happy, relieved voice.

Kristin joined us. "The grossest thing just happened," she said. "I saw Miss Scarlett in the hall, and because I've been out sick for two days, she made me stick out my tongue to see if it had white spots on it!"

I was so glad to have her interrupt Lacey that I couldn't say anything, but Elizabeth said, "Well, did it?"

"No," Kristin said, "but I was really afraid that it would have a piece of cereal or something like that on it."

Lacey looked very confused during this conversation, and the mean look on her face faltered a little. The bell rang.

"I'd better go have Mr. Wilfred sign my absence slip," Kristin said. "Come on, Lacey. Jessica, you coming?"

I swallowed. "In a minute."

"Bye, Kristin," Elizabeth said.

I could see that Lacey wanted to say something else to me, but Kristin sort of steered her into the classroom. I collapsed against Elizabeth. "Thank goodness you and Kristin were here. That could have been really bad."

"No problem," Elizabeth said. "I'll meet you after class at your locker, okay? I should run before the last bell—"

"There he is!" I interrupted, squeezing her arm. Walking down the hall right toward us was the incredibly cute guy who had rescued me yesterday.

"There who is?" Elizabeth asked in a really loud voice.

"Shhh!" I dug my fingernails into her forearm. "That guy I was asking you about yesterday. Remember?"

Elizabeth squinted. "Do you mean Damon Ross?"

Damon. The name fit him.

"Yes," I hissed. "How do you know him?"

"He's on the *Spec,*" Elizabeth said.

Just then Damon passed us. He seemed even better looking than he had the day before, if that was possible.

He looked from me to Elizabeth and then back at me. And—here's the good part—he *smiled.*

He can tell us apart! I thought dizzily. *He knows it was me yesterday!*

I twisted my neck and watched him until he was out of sight.

I had a feeling about Damon. A feeling called fate.

A n n a

"Hey, Elizabeth, headed for lunch?" I asked, catching up to her on the way to the caf.

I hadn't talked to her all morning. Elizabeth smiled. "Sorry, Anna, I can't today. I have to spend lunch hour in the library cramming for that Spanish test."

"Is it really that bad?" I asked sympathetically. "Do you need help or anything?"

She shook her head. "I'm just going to go over the vocabulary."

"I can't have lunch either," Salvador said unexpectedly from behind us. Elizabeth and I both jumped and turned. I wondered how long he had been back there.

"Hi," I said. "Why can't you have lunch?"

He rolled his eyes. "Mrs. Pomfrey gave me detention."

"What did you do?" Elizabeth and I asked in unison.

Salvador actually looked a little sheepish.

"Well, Monday when we had a substitute teacher and she called roll, I screamed, '*Here!* Oh, sorry,' after every single name."

Elizabeth and I rolled our eyes.

"If you two hadn't gotten out of English that day to help Charlie with the layouts, you would have loved it," Salvador insisted. "It was actually pretty hilarious."

Elizabeth looked at me and shook her head. Then we both laughed.

"Well, I'll see you in Spanish," Elizabeth said to me.

"Me too," Salvador said.

I smiled and waved as they walked off down the hall together. I could hear Salvador imitating Elizabeth's Spanish accent, talking slowly and flatly. She punched him on the shoulder playfully, and I felt a pang. Lunch without my two friends didn't seem very appealing.

I went to my locker and got my sandwich and a notebook. I thought I would take my lunch outside and work on a new poem. Flipping through the notebook, I bit my lip. So many of my poems were about Tim. I didn't want to think about him right now—not in the middle of the school day. I jammed the notebook back into my locker and slammed it shut. *Back to the caf*, I thought.

I stopped at the girls' room, then pushed my way through the heavy cafeteria doors. And there were Elizabeth and Salvador sitting at our usual table.

Salvador was leaning toward Elizabeth across the table, gesturing. Elizabeth, who was sitting sideways with her feet resting on another chair, had her head thrown back, laughing. She stopped laughing the second she saw me. Or maybe that was only my imagination.

"Anna!" Elizabeth said. "We didn't know where you went. Sit down." She moved her feet.

"Well, I almost didn't come here at all," I said, taking a seat. "Because I thought you guys weren't going to be here." My voice sounded snippier than I meant it to.

"On the way to the library we saw Mr. Enrico and he told us that the Spanish test is canceled," Elizabeth said. "Isn't that great?"

I nodded, trying to look like I believed her. *Don't be paranoid*, I told myself. *They aren't trying to blow you off. Salvador couldn't possibly like her better than you.*

"Apparently the Xerox machine is broken," Elizabeth went on. "And then Salvador went to Mrs. Pomfrey's room—"

"And she canceled my detention because her peptic ulcer is acting up," Salvador finished. "She said only two things make it act up, me and

79

Tabasco sauce. So she said in the interest of health . . ."

I had no idea whether they were lying to me or not.

I had seen them not five minutes ago. What were the odds of them seeing Mr. Enrico and Mrs. Pomfrey in the time it took me to go to my locker and the bathroom? And having both teachers cancel a test and a detention?

Did Salvador set the whole thing up so he and Elizabeth could have lunch alone together? I felt light-headed. *What if he did? Salvador is my best friend. What would I do if I weren't his best friend anymore? I would have to eat lunch alone forever. . . .*

My mind was reeling.

But if Salvador and Elizabeth wanted to be alone together, they could have both gone to the library, I reasoned. They wouldn't have come to the cafeteria, which was, in fact, exactly where they thought I would be. That didn't make any sense, right? Right?

"Anna?" Elizabeth said. "Are you okay?"

"Sure," I replied. "Why wouldn't I be?"

But I felt shaken.

Elizabeth smiled at me. "Hey, I know! Remember how I said you guys should come over for dinner? Well, why don't you come tonight? Can you make it?"

"Sure," Salvador said.

Elizabeth looked at me. "Anna?"

"No!" I wanted to say. "No way! I don't want to spend any more time with you and my so-called best friend!"

Elizabeth was looking at me expectantly.

Don't be so jealous, I told myself. *These are your* friends, *remember?*

"Sure," I said. "I'd love to."

Hi, Kristin!

I can't believe you were so nice to Jessica! Don't you know that we call her "Lamefield" now? Justin thought it up on Eyeball Alley when we found out that she'd been pretending her brother was her boyfriend! Isn't "Lamefield" hilarious?!?

Justin and Matt were teasing her yesterday— saying they were going to squirt shaving cream in her locker. I wasn't there, but Justin said that she started crying, so they left her alone. What a baby!

Wouldn't it be funny if *we* sprayed shaving cream through the vents in her locker?

Lacey

Lace,

It is so *not* funny that those jerks made Jessica cry. How would you feel if Justin and Matt started making fun of *you?* Why do you hang with those stupid guys anyway?

Poor Jessica. I bet this boyfriend thing was just some sort of misunderstanding.

K.

Hey, Kristin,

You're not mad at me, are you? I'll tell Justin not to do the shaving-cream thing. You're still sleeping over Friday, right?

You are so lucky you were out sick Monday! Mme. Vivienne made us sing French nursery rhymes *one at a time.* . . .

Elizabeth

I was afraid my parents would be angry that I'd invited Salvador and Anna to dinner without asking their permission first, but my dad was pretty excited about it.

"We should go out somewhere," he said. "Happy Burger, maybe? Anyway, we'd love to meet your friends."

I was excited too. I just knew that Jessica was going to love Anna and Salvador once she got to know them. *They're so smart and outgoing,* I thought. *Just the kind of people Jessica should be friends with.*

Dad looked at Jessica. "You should invite that young man," he suggested.

Jessica looked startled. "What young man?"

"The one we met at the movies," my dad said. "Al Rheece's son. Ronald."

Jessica began making noises like her stomach hurt. "Oh, Dad, please . . ."

"What?" my dad asked. "From what I hear,

he's quite a remarkable young man."

"Remarkably nerdy," Jessica said. "Remarkably weird. And if you ever invite him anywhere near this house without giving me enough warning to go somewhere else, I'll—I'll—"

Apparently Jessica couldn't think of anything dire enough to threaten Dad with, so she dropped that and said, "And another thing, if we see anyone cool at Happy Burger, pretend you're not with us."

My dad rolled his eyes, and Jessica followed me upstairs to change.

"I don't know why we have to go out with Salvador and Whatsherface anyway," she grumbled.

I was shocked. "What do you mean? I thought you wanted friends." I stared at her. "Salvador and Anna are funny. And nice. You'll like them."

Jessica gave me a look I couldn't really interpret and went into her room. Didn't she realize that I was doing this for her? I drifted into my room, thinking how great it would be if Jessica and Salvador and Anna did get along. Jessica and I had never really hung with the same crowd before. I wondered why that was.

Salvador's grandmother dropped him and Anna at our house a little before seven, and we had to divide up into two cars to go to Happy Burger. Salvador and Jessica rode with Steven while Anna and I rode with Mom and Dad.

I had thought for some reason that Anna would be shy around my parents, but she was very talkative and told them all about a dance lesson she and Salvador had taken. My parents laughed, but I felt a little pang. I don't know why because there are plenty of things Salvador and Anna do without me and usually it doesn't really bother me. But dance lessons . . . had they danced with each other? What would it be like to dance with Salvador? A slow dance—

I shook my head to clear away the thought.

When we got to Happy Burger, Steven, Jessica, and Salvador were already there, of course. Steven drives fast.

"How was the ride?" I asked, getting out of the car.

Salvador pretended to stagger. "I have seen through time," he said solemnly.

Anna giggled, but Jessica said, "What's that supposed to mean?"

"It means that I wouldn't be surprised if my hair had turned white," Salvador answered. "It means that I aged twenty years in the last"—he turned to Steven—"what was it? Three minutes?"

"Two minutes and forty seconds," Steven said, looking pleased. "A personal record."

"Thank you," Salvador said. "I didn't realize American cars came equipped with warp speed."

Everyone laughed except for Jessica, who looked annoyed. I don't know why because Steven's driving scares the heck out of her too.

We went into the restaurant, and the hostess showed us to a table. Somehow Anna wound up next to Steven, and they began chatting away. I was a little surprised because most of my friends are kind of tongue-tied around Steven unless they have teenage brothers themselves. But I know Anna is an only child.

The waiter came over to our table. "Are you folks ready to order?" He smiled at Jessica. "How about you?"

She smiled back and tilted her head so that her long, blond hair fell over one shoulder. She loves to flirt with teenage waiters, and this one was really cute. He had dark hair and eyes, like Salvador. "I don't know . . . what do you recommend?" Jessica asked.

The waiter pretended to consider. "For you? How about the Princess Burger?"

Jessica looked at him from under her eyelashes. "Maybe I—"

"Excuse me for interrupting this magic moment," Salvador said suddenly, "but I'd like the veggie burger, please."

Steven laughed, and Jessica glared at both him and Salvador. Everyone ordered, and then Steven and Anna launched into a conversation about used cars—Steven's favorite subject. I was glad that they were getting along, but I wished that they would help smooth things over between Jessica and Salvador. It was becoming more apparent to me every minute that Jessica didn't like it when anyone laughed at Salvador's jokes and Salvador didn't like it when Jessica was the center of attention.

"Are you a vegetarian, Salvador?" my dad asked as our burgers were served. "If I had known, I wouldn't have brought you to a hamburger joint."

"Oh, not really—," Salvador said. He broke off suddenly, just as Jessica was ready to take a bite of her burger. "Don't eat that!" Salvador shouted. "It's alive!"

The whole table laughed except for Jessica, who put down her burger and scowled. I rolled my eyes. Couldn't she see that Salvador was just teasing her? Jessica doesn't usually get bent when someone tries to steal the show, but Salvador was obviously rubbing her the wrong way.

The waiter came rushing over. "Is everything all right?" He saw Jessica's untouched plate. "Is your hamburger okay?"

Elizabeth

Jessica gave him her prettiest smile. "It's delicious, thank you."

I noticed that Salvador was watching the whole exchange.

"Why didn't you tell him the truth?" he asked after the waiter had left. "That you wanted a crown and scepter with your Princess Burger?"

I giggled and then felt a sharp kick on my shin. Jessica was glaring at me from across the table.

I closed my eyes. This was going to be a really long evening.

Jessica

When I woke up on Friday, I actually felt pretty optimistic. Nothing horrible had happened yesterday, not even in the cafeteria, although I'd eaten lunch with Ronald Rheece at a table in the corner. And as we were eating, two kids walked by and said, "Hey, where's your twin?" and smiled in a friendly way.

Maybe even more people would talk to me today. This twin thing was working out great.

I was feeling so happy that I hopped right out of bed before the alarm even went off. I had already taken a shower and was blow drying my hair by the time Elizabeth came into the bathroom. She yawned and smiled at me sleepily. I shouted, "Good morning, Twinnie!" over the noise of the hair dryer, and Elizabeth got into the shower.

I finished drying my hair and brushed it out. Some of Elizabeth's barrettes were lying on the bathroom counter, which gave me an idea. I

89

picked up two and carefully fastened my hair back. It looked really good—which I guess made sense because Elizabeth had been wearing her hair that way lately and it worked for her.

I smiled at myself in the mirror. People at SVJH clearly thought twins were cool. And wouldn't it be cooler if we looked even *more* alike?

Elizabeth was still in the shower, so I slipped into her room. As I knew she would, she had laid out the clothes she was going to wear to school that day: a denim skirt, white blouse, and green cardigan.

I went back to my room and rummaged through my closet. I had a denim skirt too, although it was a little shorter than Elizabeth's. A white blouse was no problem, but I couldn't find a green cardigan. Finally I chose a red one, figuring we would be dressed enough alike for people to notice, and I walked out of my room just as Elizabeth was stepping out of hers.

"Oh, shoot," she said as soon as she saw me. She put her hand back on the doorknob. "I'd better change."

"Why?" I asked quickly.

She gestured at my outfit. "Because we're dressed alike."

"But—" I hesitated. "Don't you think it would

fun to dress alike, I mean, since we happened to anyway? I think it would be cool."

She stared me. "You do?"

"Well, sure," I said, trying to sound convincing. "Come on, it'll be fun. We could—we could even switch places. All we'd have to do is trade sweaters."

Elizabeth narrowed her eyes at me. "What are you up to?"

"Nothing," I said, trying to make my face innocent.

"I don't want to switch places," Elizabeth said.

"Why not?"

"Because I just don't want to. And actually, I don't even think I want to *dress* alike. We haven't done that in a long time."

"Fine," I snapped. "Suit yourself."

"I will," she said, and turned to go back into her room.

A cold feeling settled in my stomach. *She's mad,* I thought, realizing suddenly how much I was counting on Elizabeth to make my day bearable. What would I do without her?

"I'm sorry, Elizabeth," I said meekly. "I just thought you would like the idea. I'll change."

Elizabeth softened. "Okay. Thanks, Jess."

"No sweat," I said. I went back into my room and changed into jeans and a long-sleeved green shirt. At least Elizabeth and I could both wear the same color—I didn't think she would object to that.

She didn't, and she seemed happy as we walked to the bus stop. But there was one more favor I needed from her.

"Hey, it's Friday," I said. "What are you doing tonight?"

"I have a *Spec* meeting," Elizabeth said.

"Want to do something afterward?" I asked.

"I can't," she said. "I have that dance-a-thon with Salvador and Anna."

I'd forgotten about that. What was I going to do now? The prospect of an entire weekend without any plans wasn't very appealing. "Well, can I go with you guys?"

Elizabeth raised an eyebrow. "I don't think that's such a good idea."

"Why not?"

She gave me a look. "You could have been nicer to Salvador Wednesday night."

"He could have been nicer to me!" I shot back. Then I stopped myself. "I'll be really nice to him tonight, Lizzie, I promise. Besides, it's all in the name of charity, right?"

Elizabeth hesitated. "Well, yes."

"I like the idea of dancing for charity," I coaxed. "You can have more than four people on your team, can't you?"

Elizabeth sighed. "Well, maybe . . . but how would you get there?"

"I could come to the *Spec* meeting with you," I suggested.

She looked dubious. "You want to hang out at the newspaper?"

Of course I wanted to hang out at the newspaper. More than I wanted to sit alone in my room and stare at the ceiling anyway. "Don't look so shocked, Lizzie." I gave her my best pout. "I could be interested in journalism. You're not the only smart one, you know."

"It's not that." Elizabeth bit her lip. "I just think you'll be bored. You won't really know anyone there."

"I'll know you and Salvador and Anna and—" Suddenly I realized something. "And I know Damon." Elizabeth looked at me sideways. "Well, I sort of know him," I said.

"We'll be busy," Elizabeth said shortly.

"I could just sit outside and read a book and then leave with you afterward," I offered, watching her carefully to see if she had heard the lie in my voice. Now that I realized what a big opportunity going to the *Spectator* was, I wasn't about to take no for an answer.

"Well, all right," Elizabeth said. She didn't sound too happy.

Jessica

I, on the other hand, was extremely happy and immediately started planning what I would wear.

I felt kind of bad lying to Elizabeth, but there was no way I was going to sit outside and read a book during the *Spectator* meeting. I was going to go in there and show off all of my latent newspaper talents.

Tonight I was going to spend some quality time with Damon Ross.

Elizabeth

Jessica and I ran into Brian at our locker just before lunch.

"Hey," he said, smiling at Jessica. "New hairdo?"

"Yes." She batted her eyes.

I hadn't really been paying attention, but now I noticed that Jessica was wearing her hair back in barrettes. I was kind of surprised since I'd always thought she hated that style.

"What are you guys talking about?" a voice behind us demanded.

We jumped and turned around. Salvador and Anna were standing there.

"Hi, guys!" I said warmly.

"Hello, El Salvador," Jessica said, and rolled her eyes.

Lacey Frells picked that moment to walk by. Kristin wasn't with her, and I wondered whether she was going to say anything nasty to Jessica. Well, if so, she was going to get chewed out—by me. I glanced at my sister and saw her exchange a look with Lacey.

Lacey gave a slight sneer, then looked around at all of us. She walked past without saying a word.

"Ha!" Jessica said as soon as Lacey was out of earshot. "Did you see that?" She grinned at me. "Did you?"

I nodded.

"See what?" Salvador asked.

"None of your business, El Salvador," Jessica replied. "Just a little something that made putting up with *you* worthwhile."

"Wow, I wonder what that could be," he mused. "Did you finally take note of my fantastic personality?"

"Right. Well, I've got to get to class!" Jessica said, giving us a slight wave and taking off down the hall. "Bye, everyone."

"Good-bye," Brian said, waving after her.

Anna and Salvador were silent.

"So, are you guys ready for tonight?" Brian asked.

"Oh, you mean the dance-a-thon?" I said. I took a deep breath. "Actually, I have to talk to you guys about that. Jessica really wants to come with us, and I said she could. I hope that was okay."

"It's okay with me," Anna said.

"Why not?" Brian asked. "The more the merrier."

"You're so nice to come to this," I told him.

"You weren't even screwing around in class—we were."

"Yeah," Anna put in. "I can't believe you didn't demand a trial by jury, Brian."

Brian laughed. "Miss Scarlett just wanted four volunteers. If it hadn't been you guys, it would have been me and three other people. She knows I'm a pushover."

"You're too much of a sweetie," I said lightly.

"He's not *that* nice," Salvador said, kind of harshly. We all looked at him in surprise and he added, "You just don't know Brian's dark side yet, Elizabeth."

Brian and I laughed, but Anna gave Salvador a weird look.

"Lunch?" I asked, holding mine up.

"Lunch," Salvador confirmed, and the four of us headed to the cafeteria.

Jessica and Salvador will learn to get along, I told myself. I prayed that it was true.

"Hi, the del Valles' answering machine is broken. This is their refrigerator speaking. Please leave a message."

Beep.

"Hello, you've reached the Wakefield residence, and we're pleased to announce that Steven has been adopted into a new family and can no longer be reached at this num—argh! Steven, give me that! *Steven!*"

Beep.

"Hi, this Lacey. Please leave a message and then wait by your phone until I call you back."

Beep.

"Greetings, you are communicating with the voice-mail system of the Wang family. Following this recording, there will be a medium-pitched sine wave, which is your signal to begin your message. Please be concise."

Beep.

[*In a monster voice*] "Hi, this is Brian Rainey, and I'm not myself right now . . ." [*Horror-movie laughter*]

Beep.

"Hello, Wakefield residence. Unfortunately Jessica is in traction right now and will be unable to receive calls until Christmas. We're all really broken up about it. If this is Kathy, I'll pick you up at eight."

Beep.

"Hi, this is Anna, and if anyone called earlier and heard my dad's supernerdy outgoing message, please don't think less of us."

Beep.

"Hi, this is Margie and Kristin Seltzer, and we're screening our calls. At the beep start talking, and if we pick up, it means we're willing to talk to you. If we don't, we're not home."

Beep.

"Hello, you have reached the abode of Alphonse Fox. Please be so kind as to leave a message at the beep."

Beep.

Elizabeth

Charlie was just unlocking the journalism room when we got to the school that night. My twin wasted no time. She marched right up and asked Charlie if she could "sit in" on the *Spec* meeting.

"What happened to your book?" I asked.

"No outsiders," Charlie said automatically.

"I'm just so fascinated by journalism," Jessica told her.

"You are?" I asked. "Since when?"

Jessica ignored me. "Especially in the way you lead the meeting, Charlie," she went on. "You have so much style."

I could see Charlie was wavering, and I gave up trying to protest. Jessica usually got what she wanted, and she wanted to sit in on this meeting, for whatever reason.

Charlie held open the door and Jessica barreled inside. Anna came up to me and whispered, "I thought your sister was going to stay outside."

"Me too," I whispered back.

One we were inside, everyone scattered around the room to work on their various projects. Some people were on the computers, some were using graph paper to set type, and some were doing page layouts, but everyone was busy at something.

Everyone except for Jessica, that is, who lounged against Charlie's desk—I mean, Mr. Desmond's desk—and said, "Where's Damon?"

Charlie was scanning a piece of paper. "Who?"

"Damon Ross," Jessica repeated. "Cute, tall, likes to rescue damsels in distress?"

"Damon asked to be excused from the meeting," Charlie said in a bored voice. "I don't know where he is."

Jessica looked horrified. "Do you mean he's not going to be here at all—Liz, what are you doing?"

I had an iron grip on Jessica's arm.

"Damon Ross?" I hissed, pulling her away from the desk. "I thought this was all in the name of charity!"

Jessica pouted at me. "I'm just trying to make friends, Lizzie," she whispered.

I sighed. "All right," I replied. "But you still can't disrupt the meeting." I marched her over to a desk at the front of the room. "Now, sit here," I said. "And be quiet."

Jessica slouched into the chair and began picking at her nails sulkily. I walked back over to Salvador and Anna, who were piecing together a layout for one of the advertising pages.

"Sorry," I murmured.

They gave me sympathetic looks, and I was glad that they weren't angry or embarrassed. I sure was! I should have known Jessica wouldn't sit outside and read a book. The last book she read was one that was being passed all around school with the dirty parts underlined.

I sat down at one of the free computers. I took out the notes from my interview with Mrs. Fransky, looked them over, and started typing.

> Mrs. Eileen Fransky, who retires from Sweet Valley Junior High this year after more than forty-five years of teaching home economics, says that she'll be sad to go. "This has been my life's work," Mrs. Fransky says. "But this meeting is sure boring. Are you sure

I looked up suddenly.

"Are you sure Damon isn't going to show up?" Jessica was asking Charlie.

"Jessica!" I said warningly. "Sorry, Charlie," I added.

Jessica glared at me but quieted down.

I reread what I'd just typed and realized that I hadn't been quoting Mrs. Fransky—I'd been quoting what Jessica had said to Charlie. Annoyed, I deleted what I had written and started over.

I wasn't too thrilled with what I had typed anyway, so I decided to start with a new approach.

Mrs. Eileen Fransky's clam dip is something to rave about, and she owes it all to her husband. "It's kind of a funny story," Mrs. Fransky says. "But couldn't we turn on the radio or something? Don't you do anything but work? No wonder all the articles are so boring

"Jess!" I snapped, looking up.

She glanced at me, and I mouthed, "Shut up!" as distinctly as possible.

Charlie looked at Jessica and said in a very cool voice, "If you want to make yourself useful—"

"I don't particularly—," Jessica started.

"—you can type up this article I wrote about the new swimming pool," Charlie finished. She handed Jessica a piece of yellow legal paper.

Jessica sighed and flounced down the aisle to the computer next to me.

Elizabeth

"Just type," I whispered. "No more talking!"

She rolled her eyes at me but began typing. Jessica is strictly a two-finger typist, so that one page kept her busy for the rest of the meeting. Thankfully. I kept stealing glances at Salvador and Anna, but they didn't look up. In a way, I was glad they were busy. I didn't want them to think less of Jessica just because she didn't know how to act at the newspaper. Really, this was all *my* fault. I never should have let her come in the first place.

Finally, finally, Charlie wrapped up the meeting. Jessica gave a huge sigh of relief. She was so embarrassing. How rude!

I managed to finish my article on Mrs. Fransky and was just packing up my stuff when I heard Charlie start yelling.

"What are you talking about?" she stormed at Jessica, waving a sheet of paper. "There was 'no mysterious fish possibly believed to be a piranha found in the wading pool'!"

"I'm just trying to increase sales," Jessica replied. "Someday you'll thank me—"

I grabbed the collar of Jessica's shirt and propelled her out into the hall, where Salvador, Anna, and Brian Rainey were waiting.

"Hi, Elizabeth," Brian said. "My mom is waiting for us in the car."

"Wow," Jessica said, fluffing her hair as we walked to the car. "That meeting was even more boring than I ever dreamed it could be."

I closed my eyes. *She's my sister and I love her,* I reminded myself. I repeated it silently all the way to the dance-a-thon. *She's my sister and I love her. She's my sister and I love her. She's my sister and I love her. . . .*

A n n a

There was a line for dance-team registration just outside the community-center gymnasium. Brian, Elizabeth, and her sister went to register us. Salvador disappeared somewhere, and I peered into the gym.

I could see why Salvador hadn't liked the dance he went to here. The gym was dark and smelled even more like sweat socks than the one at school. The only decoration was a banner that read, Remember! You're Dancing for Their Lives! It was kind of creepy.

Salvador reappeared by my side. "I checked out the entertainment."

"Well?" I raised my eyebrows. "Is it the marching band again?"

Salvador shook his head. "No, they have somebody's dad acting as deejay."

I folded my arms across my chest. "How do you know it's somebody's dad?"

He grinned. "Come look for yourself."

He grabbed my elbow and led me through the dancers to the deejay table. A man in headphones, wearing a sweater vest and bifocals, was standing behind the twin turntables. He was squinting at an album cover. "And now," he said into his microphone, "we have something from the Space Girls!"

"Translation: Spice Girls," Salvador whispered. His mouth tickled my ear, and I giggled.

I nodded. "You're right. It's someone's dad."

We went back to the lobby, where Elizabeth and the others were looking for us. I was feeling really happy. Salvador and I had spent a lot of time working together at the *Spec,* and it had been totally normal. *You have nothing to be jealous about,* I thought. *Nothing has changed.* For the first time in a long while, I believed it.

Brian handed us each a blue armband. "We're the turquoise team."

Jessica frowned. "This clashes with my outfit."

Everyone ignored her.

"They gave us a list of rules," Elizabeth said. She handed me a piece of paper, and I held it out so that all five of us could read it.

Hospital Dance-a-thon Rules

Please read the following seven rules carefully. Violation of any of these rules will result in members of your team having to pay five dollars out of their own pockets to the hospital.

Arguing with the referees can result in your team being disqualified.

Rule #1: Please wear proper attire. No miniskirts. All shirts must be tucked in.

"We haven't even started and I already broke a stupid rule," Jessica said. "I can't tuck my shirt in. It's not long enough."

Jessica was really starting to annoy me. I guess she was starting to annoy Salvador too because he opened his mouth to say something.

"It's okay, Jessica," Elizabeth put in quickly. "If you just sort of slouch, nobody will be able to see your stomach."

Jessica flipped her hair over her shoulder, apparently not interested in Elizabeth's fashion advice. Now I was irritated with both of them. Why did Elizabeth have to spend so much time trying to take care of her sister? And why did Jessica have to be so rude? I had managed to ignore her when we were at the *Spec,* but I didn't know how long I could keep it up now that we were all going to be dancing together.

I liked Elizabeth, but I was starting to wonder

whether being her friend was worth the price of hanging with her twin.

Brian said something in a low voice to Elizabeth, and she laughed.

Salvador frowned and stuck his head between them. "What did you say?" he asked Brian.

Brian looked startled. "I just said that I didn't know you could bodysurf without water."

Salvador turned to Elizabeth. "And what did you say?"

"I didn't say anything," Elizabeth replied. "I laughed."

"Oh." Salvador bit his lip and looked at Elizabeth.

"I hope they play some good music so I can show off my moves," Brian said, doing an awkward little spin.

I laughed, but Salvador said, "I'm a pretty good dancer too." He was looking at Elizabeth when he said it, but when I let out a snort, he turned and glared at me.

"Sorry," I told him quickly. I felt guilty for snorting at his dancing ability like that.

"Come with me to check out the refreshments," I said, grabbing Salvador's hand.

"I—I'm not really hungry," he hedged, looking from Elizabeth to Brian and back at Elizabeth again.

"I'll come, Anna," Elizabeth volunteered.

"Well, if we're all going," Salvador said, "I'll come along." He dropped my hand.

Suddenly I didn't want to go anymore. *He does like her,* I thought. I felt sick, and all I wanted was for Elizabeth and Salvador to get away from me before I started screaming. "Why don't you guys go ahead?" I suggested in as calm a voice as I could manage. "I'll stay here, and Brian can teach me his moves."

"Okay!" Salvador said.

"Don't you want to come?" Elizabeth asked. She looked kind of confused, and I couldn't exactly blame her.

I turned to Salvador and looked him in the eye. "No," I said, "thanks." He dropped his gaze. *That's right, look away,* I told him silently. *You fake. You* liar.

"All right." Elizabeth sighed. "Let's go, Salvador." He looked up at her and smiled, and they walked to the far corner of the gym.

"Salvador's acting kind of weird," Brian remarked.

"No kidding," I replied. I looked down at the list of rules that was still in my hand. Jessica had already broken the first one, and my best friend was replacing me.

This evening was not looking good.

> Rule #2: There will be one rest period of five minutes after every fifty-five minutes danced.

The referee blows his whistle at Brian. "No resting."

"I'm not resting," Brian protests. "I'm just dancing very slowly."

> Rule #3: No food or drink consumed on the dance floor.

"No food or drink, buddy," a referee says to Salvador. "Get rid of that chewing gum."

"Since when is chewing gum a food?" Salvador asks Anna. "Can you tell me which of the four food groups it belongs to?"

> Rule #4: No body bashing, body surfing, or other potentially harmful behavior.

Anna, in attempting to demonstrate a dance step to Brian, loses her balance and succeeds in body surfing without even knowing what it was.

> Rule #5: No colliding with other dancers.

During a slow dance Elizabeth dances with Brian, and Salvador is so busy watching them that he and Anna collide with another couple, creating a (in Salvador's opinion, at least) very amusing domino effect.

Rule #6: Only your feet may touch the dance floor. No sitting, kneeling, or crawling.

The referee spots Elizabeth crawling, blows his whistle, and makes a mark on his clipboard. Salvador moans. "What were you doing?"

"I was looking for my earring," Elizabeth replies.

Rule #7: No toilet trips except during rest periods.

A referee puts his hand on Jessica's arm as she attempts to leave the gym. "Where do you think you're going, miss?"

"To the bathroom."

"It's not a rest period."

"Look, do you want a puddle on the floor or not?" Jessica asks.

Elizabeth

"Do you want a puddle on the floor or not?" Jessica asked the referee again. "Because if you don't, you're going to have to let go of my arm in the next ten seconds."

She's my sister and I love her, I reminded myself, although my patience with Jessica was really wearing thin at this point.

"Are you arguing with me?" The ref's face was thunderous. "Because that is grounds for disqualification."

I stepped forward quickly. "It's okay—she can go," I said to the referee. "We're willing to take the rule violation."

The ref hesitated, then nodded. He released Jessica's arm and made a mark on his clipboard.

As soon as he had moved away, Salvador danced over and said, "I can't believe you did that, Jessica!"

"What are you talking about?" Jessica demanded. "You've already broken a bunch of rules, so I don't know why you're jumping all over me."

"Come on, guys," I said, but they ignored me.

Anna and Brian were dancing nearby, listening to the argument. I kept swaying too, even though it was hard when all I wanted to do was strangle my sister. But we didn't need any more rule violations.

"*I* didn't break any rules that could get us disqualified—," Salvador started.

"No, just ones that cost us money," Jessica snapped. "I'm sick of you acting like a know-it-all."

"Well, I'm sick of you acting like a selfish little jerk," Salvador snapped right back.

Jessica narrowed her eyes. "That's it!" She pointed a finger in his face. "I've had it with you, El Salvador, and with this dumb dance, and with everything else!"

I was feeling sick. "Jess, please—," I started.

"And if you think I'm going to stick around here and let you insult me, you're totally, totally wrong!" Jessica finished. She turned to me. "Come on, Lizzie. Let's go. We can call Steven for a ride."

What? I stared at her in shock. I hadn't even wanted her to come with us tonight, and now Jessica wanted me to just ditch my friends? "Jessica, be reasonable," I pleaded.

"I have been reasonable!" Jessica was practically

shouting now. "And now I want to go home!"

I took a deep breath, not believing what I was hearing. Reasonable? Jessica had horned her way in on our plans and made all sorts of promises about staying out of the way and being nice to Salvador and she hadn't kept any of them!

I didn't have the slightest desire to turn my back on my friends and walk out with her. But I knew what not going with her meant. It meant that we would never hang with the same group of friends. It meant that we were going our own ways. And it meant that I hadn't solved Jessica's problem. She would still be lonely in our new school. And Lacey would still be horrible. My heart ached for her, but I couldn't fix everything this time.

"No, Jess," I said finally. "You go if you want to, but I'm staying here."

Jessica's eyes got very wide. I realized that she had asked me to come with her only as a formality. She had expected I would.

"Fine," she spat, turning on her heel and stalking out of the gymnasium.

I watched her go, blinking back tears. I hate it when Jessica is angry with me. *I can't help it if she doesn't like my friends,* I reminded myself, but I still felt miserable.

Salvador, still dancing, came over to me. "I'm

sorry," he said. "She's right. I do always pick on her. Do you want me to go after her and apologize?"

I gave him a small smile. "No. It's okay. I think it's probably better this way."

The music ended suddenly, and we all stood there for a moment in silence. Then Brian said, "You know, by my calculations, we owe the hospital more money than my allowance adds up to in a month, and I'm already exhausted."

We all laughed, and Anna smiled at me. "Don't worry about Jessica. She'll come around."

I nodded. "I know. She has to—she's my sister."

Just then a slow dance started. Brian bowed to Anna. "May I have this dance?" he asked.

She nodded and laughed.

"If I fall asleep on your shoulder," Brian added, "just ignore it. I'll try not to drool on you."

I watched them waltz off together and smiled a little bit. I was lucky to have friends like and Anna and Brian . . . and Salvador.

I turned to Salvador now. He was looking at me with a strange expression on his face. I didn't know what else to say, so I just asked him, "Do you want to dance?"

Jessica

"Can you come pick me up at the community center?" I asked the minute Steven picked up the phone.

"Absolutely no problem," he said. "Be there in a flash."

I was sort of surprised by that since Steven doesn't usually like to be treated as a car service, but I found out later that Kathy had canceled their date. Steven was stuck doing his economics homework and would have agreed to pick up a total stranger from the South Pole just to have a break.

I went outside to wait for Steven and smolder some more about Salvador. Why did Elizabeth always pick the most annoying people to be friends with? *I put up with a lot from Salvador,* I thought, *and the paper!* I had tried and tried to be nice and helpful at the *Spec,* but I just couldn't act like Elizabeth all the time—I didn't know how! Didn't Elizabeth realize how hard I was trying? Didn't she *care?* I still couldn't believe I had wasted my time hanging out with all her boring friends.

Still . . . hadn't hanging with Elizabeth's buds been better than having no friends at all? Now I was going to have to go back to being Jessica Lamefield. Which was worse?

The glass doors opened behind me, and I turned automatically to face them. My breath caught in my throat.

It was Damon Ross.

He was coming carefully out the heavy doors, leading a little girl by the hand. Another, even smaller girl was nestled in his arms. Both girls had wet hair.

"Okay, Kaia," Damon said softly. "We're going home now. Mom will be here soon."

I hesitated a moment, then stepped forward so I wasn't in the shadows. "Hi, Damon."

He looked up, startled, and then smiled briefly. "Hi, Elizabeth."

Damon immediately turned his attention back to the little girls. "Do you want me to carry you too?" he asked the girl whose hand he was holding.

I was speechless. He still thought I was Elizabeth? But I had been so sure that he could tell us apart! That look he gave me in the hall—I had been so certain that he knew me!

Damon and the little girls were walking past me.

I couldn't take it anymore! I was sick of being known as "Lacey's friend" or "Elizabeth's sister." Didn't *anyone* care that I had a personality too? "Not Elizabeth," I said loudly. "I'm Jessica."

Damon paused and then turned. He looked at me for a moment, his head tilted. "I thought you were Elizabeth with your hair pulled back like that."

I shook my head, suddenly shy.

Damon adjusted the little girl he was holding. "These are my sisters," he said. "Sally and Kaia is the baby. This is Jessica Wakefield," he told them.

"Hi," I said, walking over to them. Sally smiled up at me.

"They wanted to go swimming, and it's free night here," Damon said. "They're not usually out this late."

The baby, Kaia, reached out for the barrette in my hair. I laughed, unhooked the barrette, and handed it to her. My hair fell forward, and I tucked it behind my ear. I unfastened the other barrette and put it in my pocket.

"Whoops," Damon said, prying the barrette out of Kaia's fingers. She had started to chew on it. "I better give this back to you before she destroys it." He glanced at me and then away. "I like your hair better like that," he said softly.

119

Jessica

Before I could say anything, two cars pulled up to the curb. One was my dad's, with Steven at the wheel, and the other was a battered old sedan.

"Oh, my ride's here," Damon said.

"Mine too," I said.

Still, we stood there on the sidewalk looking at each other until Steven honked.

"Well, I'd better go," I said, backing toward the car.

Damon nodded.

I walked backward all the way to the car and then climbed inside. Steven may have said something to me. He may have talked all the way home; I have no idea.

I didn't hear a word he said.

Salvador

How can I describe dancing with Elizabeth?

I can tell you what it was like to dance with other people. The Doña, for instance. She made me slow dance with her once at a wedding, and it was like trying to hold on to a Mexican jumping bean because she was so excited in case the band played a rumba next.

At another wedding, when I was ten, I danced with my cousin's friend. All during the dance she kept stroking my head and saying to other couples, "Isn't he adorable? Look at my little boyfriend!" It was excruciating.

I had danced with Mr. Fox, but that was more like a trip to the dentist or something because Mr. Fox was very professional and didn't care if you stepped on his toes and you knew he had danced with about three thousand other people.

And, of course, I had danced with Anna. But dancing with Anna is like, I don't know . . .

curling up in your favorite chair. Or maybe stepping into the kitchen when it's cold outside. It was nice. It was easy.

But dancing with Elizabeth wasn't like dancing with any of those people. For one thing, she was taller than Anna and the Doña but shorter than Mr. Fox, so our faces were on the same level.

Also, she made me extremely conscious of my feet. My feet had been behaving themselves perfectly all evening. Well, except for when I crashed into that couple. But now, suddenly, you would think my feet had never danced before— they couldn't keep a beat. And they kept stepping on Elizabeth's toes.

I was trying to count under my breath, the way Mr. Fox had taught me—even though Elizabeth and I weren't waltzing; we were turning in circles. But my counting sounded something like this: "One, two, ouch! . . . One, two, sorry! . . . One, two, whoops! . . ."

Finally we just slowed to a shuffle, which was probably safest. But then my hands started to sweat. Well, "sweat" is putting it mildly. The hand that was on Elizabeth's back was sticking to her shirt, and I wondered how long it would be before she could feel it against her skin. And the hand that Elizabeth was holding was even worse. I was afraid to look it for fear I would see droplets of water dripping onto the floor.

Elizabeth was a good sport, though. She didn't say anything for a few minutes while my palm went on making a lake in her hand. Then, very gently, she took my hand and placed it on her back and put both her arms around my neck.

This brought our faces even closer together, and I rested my cheek against her hair. I closed my eyes and reminded myself to breathe.

When I opened my eyes again, I looked across the room—at Anna.

She was staring at me with this look on her face. I've seen it before. It was something like hurt—and anger, maybe. Anna can be really tough sometimes. But this time it was directed at *me. In the eight years we've been friends, Anna's never looked at me like that,* I thought, a sinking feeling settling in my stomach. Something in Anna's face made me remember with a jolt that Elizabeth and I were supposed to be just friends.

"What's wrong?" Elizabeth asked.

"Nothing," I lied. I realized then that I had been doing exactly what I had wanted to avoid doing with Elizabeth. Falling for her.

I looked down at Elizabeth, then back at Anna, who frowned at me.

Anna knows, I realized suddenly. *And she's mad.*

I had to do something.

123

I reached for Elizabeth's hand and lifted it into a tango pose. She laughed as we tangoed across the gym floor to Brian and Anna. I tried to dip Elizabeth and narrowly avoided dropping her on her head. So much for suave. Pulling Elizabeth upright again, I turned to Anna and asked in my most debonair voice, "Mind if I cut in?"

Anna cocked an eyebrow. "Go ahead."

I grinned at her, dropped Elizabeth's hands, and grabbed Brian and spun him around. This got a huge laugh out of everyone, just as I had hoped it would.

"No offense, man," Brian said, "but I'd like to do the leading, if you don't mind."

"Well, maybe I'd better dance with this one instead," I replied. I grinned at Anna and took her by the hand. "We've had some practice."

I glanced over at Elizabeth to see if she minded that we were changing partners. She didn't seem to. She smiled at Brian, and they danced off. It took all of my self-control not to run after them and shove them apart, saying, "No! Wait! I was only kidding!"

I didn't do it, though, and Anna and I fell into the box step.

She looked up at me. "Are you finished acting weird, then?" she asked.

Her question caught me off guard. "What—what do you mean?" As if I didn't know.

"You've been a little peculiar lately," she said. "And I've really missed my best friend."

I looked her in the eye and resolved to get over Elizabeth, one way or the other. I couldn't be a freak forever.

"Yes," I said to Anna. "I'm finished."

Dear Stupid Diary,

Okay, how lame is this? Here I am, sitting in my room—*by myself*—writing in my diary. Now I really do feel like Jessica Lamefield.

I can't believe Lizzie is still at that dance. When is she coming home?

At least this night wasn't a total disaster. What total luck that I ran into Damon. He's so—*amazing*. How cool do you have to be to make Justin and Matt totally scared of you? Ha, ha—just remembering their faces that day they ran away from Damon makes me smile.

The cool crowd isn't all that anyway. Who is Lacey to think she's so great? She uses the worst lip gloss in the world! Damon is way cooler than she is.

Ugh. Lizzie's *still* not home! This is like that whole watched-pot-boiling thing.

Well, good. I'm *glad* she isn't home. I'm still mad at her. I can't believe she stayed behind at the dancey thing with Salvador. He's so *lame!!!* How could she have chosen *him* over *me?*

It's *crazy!!!!!!!!!!!!!!!*

I can't believe she said I wasn't being reasonable!

Okay, *maybe* I should have been quieter at the newspaper.

And *maybe* I shouldn't have argued with that judge.

Maybe I shouldn't have yelled at Salvador.

Actually, I feel kind of bad about that. I mean, he is Lizzie's friend and all. Even if he is pathetic.

And she is still my sister. I guess she was trying

to do me a favor by letting me come to the dancey thing. Some favor!

Still, it was nice of her, even though it didn't work out.

Well, Salvador's a jerk. I don't like him, and I probably never will.

But Elizabeth's my twin. I guess I don't have to love her friends in order to love *her.*

I wish she would come home.

Elizabeth

When Mrs. Rainey came to pick us up from the dance-a-thon, we actually had to borrow twenty dollars from her to pay for all our rule violations. She was extremely nice about it, though, and said since it was for charity, we didn't have to pay her back.

Truthfully, I wasn't paying that much attention because I was still thinking about dancing with Salvador. It had been so different from dancing with Brian. And even though he's a much better dancer than Salvador, it wasn't the same. Salvador made me laugh and he made me get a cold feeling in the pit of my stomach all at the same time. I didn't even mind when he stepped on my feet.

But the minute Mrs. Rainey dropped me off, all thoughts of Salvador flew out of my mind. I walked slowly to the front door, not eager to face Jessica. Knowing Jessica, she would be furious that I hadn't walked out of the dance with her.

I went inside and said hello to my mom and

dad, who were in the living room, watching TV.

"Hi, honey," my mom said. "Did you have a good time?"

I nodded.

"Want to watch *The Beast with Five Fingers* on the late movie?" my dad asked. "It starts in fifteen minutes."

"Maybe," I said. "Where's Jessica?"

"I think she's upstairs," my mom said.

I went upstairs cautiously and knocked on Jessica's door. There was no answer, and my heart sank. Had she gone to sleep furious with me? But when I went into my own room, I saw a light under the bathroom door.

"Jess?"

"Come in."

Her voice sounded normal, and I pushed open the door.

Jessica was standing in front of the mirror, brushing her hair.

"Are you doing that hundred-nightly-strokes thing?" I asked tentatively.

"Yeah," she said, turning sideways. "I can never keep it up for more than a night or two, though. But I've decided to wear my hair loose. I got sick of wearing it back in two barrettes."

"Really?" I said.

Jessica stopped brushing and nodded. "I can't

stand the way it feels. After a couple of hours I felt like my eyebrows were slowly sliding up my forehead."

I smiled, and she met my eyes in the mirror for the first time.

"Did you have a good time tonight?" Jessica asked in a small voice.

I thought about it for a minute. "Yes," I said.

Jessica didn't seem very happy with that answer, but at least it was honest. I did have a good time with my friends—once Jessica had left. I mean, I loved hanging out with Jessica. But from now on, I could do that on a one-on-one basis.

And maybe that's the way it's supposed to be, I thought. Maybe you were supposed to have your own life and your own friends and then come home to your family—and in my case, my own built-in best friend.

"Hey," I said. "Do you want to watch the late movie with Mom and Dad? It's *The Beast with Five Fingers.*"

"Really?" Jessica said. "But Mom always freaks out at scary movies."

"Uh-huh."

"Oh, let's go watch, then," Jessica said, and we smiled at each other in the mirror.

I took the barrettes out of my hair. "I like it this way too," I said, looking at my reflection. "I don't have to have the same hairstyle all the time."

Jessica looked at me. "But it's an easy way for people to tell us apart."

"True," I admitted. "But everyone who really knows us can always tell us apart anyway."

Jessica laughed. "That's true too. I guess we really are pretty different."

The Secret of Clam Dip
by Elizabeth Wakefield

Mrs. Eileen Fransky has taught home economics at Sweet Valley Junior High for more than
forty-five years. She retires this year, and before
she goes, she has chosen to reveal to this reporter
something she has kept secret for more than
forty-two of those years: her clam-dip recipe.

"The first time I made it was an accident,
really," Mrs. Fransky recalls. "My husband—my
first husband—had called from work and announced at the very last minute that he was
bring some work colleagues home for cocktails
and hors d'oeuvres."

This was in the late 1950s and, according to
Mrs. Fransky, "You didn't just tell your husband
to get lost, no matter how much you wanted to. I
felt it was my duty to whip up a little something."

The only problem was that Mrs. Fransky had
nothing in the house. "I thought I might make oyster
dip," she recalls, "but all I had was an old can of
clams. So I chopped them up and added some cream
cheese, but it was really terribly bland. I kept adding
things, but nothing was giving it the proper zip."

Mrs. Fransky was at that time just a beginning home-economics teacher, but she thought
she had a flair for cooking. "The only thing in
the cupboard was some chocolate syrup. I added
two tablespoons and hoped for the best."

The result? "It was fantastic!" Mrs. Fransky says, still delighting in her triumph. "The guests ate every last morsel and one man even licked the bowl, which I thought was very complimentary even if it wasn't terribly well mannered."

One year later Mrs. Fransky entered her clam-dip recipe in the National Dip 'n' Spread contest and won first place—a prize worth more than a thousand dollars.

"That was a great deal of money in those days," Mrs. Fransky said. "And really I have my husband to thank for it, though I never admitted that to him."

Every year Mrs. Fransky serves her special clam dip to her home-economics classes and asks if they can identify the mystery ingredient. No one ever has. But now, for the first time, Mrs. Fransky has decided to put her clam-dip recipe into print as a going-away present to the students of SVJH:

Eileen's Clam Zip-Dip
1 4-ounce can of clams
1 8-ounce package of cream cheese
1 1/2 cups mayonnaise
1 tablespoon lemon juice
1/4 teaspoon hot sauce
2 tablespoons chocolate syrup

Chop clams and mix all ingredients well. Slip into something comfortable and serve with vegetables or crackers.

Jessica

On Saturday, I woke up and felt like a huge burden had been lifted from my shoulders. It took me a moment to figure out why I felt like that. Then I realized that from now on, I wasn't going to have to be nice to Lacey, or try to be Elizabeth's other half, or hang out with El Salvador and Whatsherface. I could just be myself. None of that junk had worked for me anyway.

And what's the point of being popular if you don't get along with the people you're hanging with?

Besides, I had a feeling I would have a cool new friend very soon. Damon.

This thought put me in such a good mood that I sang in the shower and kept on humming even as I ate my oatmeal.

Just as I was finishing breakfast, my mom asked me if I would go to the butcher store and pick up some chicken breasts because she was having people over for dinner.

"Why don't you make Elizabeth go?" I asked, putting on my best pout. "She's not doing anything, and I'm still eating."

"Because I went to the dry cleaners for her," Elizabeth said.

"Well, I went to the pharmacy!" I shot back, even though that was three months ago. It was nice not to have to worry about being supersweet to my sister just so I could use her as a safety shield.

Unfortunately I lost the argument and had to go to the butcher store. Actually, I didn't mind so much. It was a nice day for a bike ride.

My mom followed me to the door, giving me money and some instructions. "Now, tell the butcher that I wanted the plumpest, juiciest breasts he's got," Mom said.

I couldn't believe my mom actually thought I was going to say that! "Sure, Mom," I lied.

"I mean it," she said. "Last time he gave us some very stringy ones."

"Okay, okay," I said.

"Thanks, honey." She gave me a kiss on the cheek.

I got on my bike and pedaled to the butcher store. It was only about a fifteen-minute bike ride, but of course, there was this huge long line spilling out of the door. Just as I took my place at the end of it, Lacey and Kristin walked in.

I couldn't believe it! I actually thought about hiding behind the cash register or something, but Kristin called out, "Oh, hi, Jessica!" and I figured it was a free country and I had every bit as much right to be there as they did. Besides, what did I care what Lacey thought? I wasn't even sure I liked her.

Kristin and Lacey came and stood behind me in line.

Lacey had a sour look on her face. "What are you doing here, L—"

"Looking for something good for dinner?" Kristin finished before Lacey could use my nickname. Kristin gave Lacey a look that made her shut her mouth with a snap.

I smiled uncomfortably. "I'm buying some chicken breasts for my mom. She thinks this is the best butcher in town."

Kristin nodded sympathetically. "We're running an errand for Lacey's stepmom."

Lacey didn't say anything. The line shuffled forward a little bit. The silence stretched out. I wondered what Elizabeth would say if she were in this situation.

I decided I had no idea and might as well just say whatever I wanted to.

I turned to Lacey and Kristin and whispered,

"My mom told me to ask the butcher for the plumpest, juiciest breasts he has, but I'd sooner kill myself."

Lacey's lips twisted into an ironic smile. "My stepmom said that I should be sure to ask for *hand*-carved ham."

"What does she think he's going to carve it with?" Kristin asked. "His foot?"

All three of us started laughing and we couldn't stop, not even when I got to the front of the line and the butcher said, "What can I get for you?"

My voice was really high and squeaky from laughing so hard, so I could barely say, "Seven chicken . . . breasts, please, the plumpest ones. . . ."

We collapsed into giggles again, and the butcher just rolled his eyes. He wrapped up my chicken breasts and then he carved Lacey's ham (with his hand, even though she didn't ask).

We went outside and walked over to the bike rack.

"Which way are you going?" Kristin asked. She and Lacey had their bikes too.

"I'm just going up to Sunset and then onto Garth," I said.

"We can ride with you to Sunset," Kristin volunteered.

We set off together, and I had an idea. "Hey, do either of you know where Damon Ross lives?"

Kristin shook her head. "I don't. Do you, Lace?"

"Nobody knows anything about him," Lacey said. "He never tells anyone anything."

"Oh?" I said, intrigued. "Maybe he has some big secret."

"Really?" Lacey said. "Like what?"

I was a little surprised that she was interested. "Maybe he's in the witness protection program and can't tell anyone about himself," I suggested.

Lacey must not have realized I was kidding because her eyes got wide and she said, "Oh, I hadn't thought of that."

I smiled to myself. "Here's my turn," I said. "See you Monday."

"See you Monday," Kristin repeated.

I thought Lacey wasn't going to say anything, but just before I was out of earshot, she called, "Bye, Wakefield."

I waved.

Garth Street is a long, straight street with a hill in the middle. I biked to the top of the hill and then took my hands off the handlebars and coasted down the other side, my arms held wide.

It was almost like flying.

Check out the **all-new**....

Sweet Valley Web site—

www.sweetvalley.com

New Features

Cool Prizes

The
ONLY
official
Web site!

Hot Links

And much more!